Mental
Seeing Through the Fog

By
Kendall Belvedere Helmly

ISBN

Paperback: 978-1-965560-82-2

Hardcover: 978-1-965560-81-5

About the Author

Kendall B. Helmly was born and raised in a middle-income suburban setting. Dad was a university STEM professor. Mom was a housewife. One car and one dog growing up in a neighborhood with many children to share aspirations with. Later in life, the desire to write became an obsession. Starting as an amateur poet and graduating to fiction writing, Kendall expresses both the grit and passion of the human experience through storytelling.

"Words have power, good and bad. One's psyche is influenced by their interpretation. Through literature, we experience a silent world of idioms, and freedom of choice reveals our version of the truth."

Dedicated to Family Evermore.

Contents

Chapter 1: Seeing Through the Fog

We sat on the school bus, just staring at each other. Finally, I got the courage to sit next to Susan. The bus came to a halt at Susan's stop, and I decided to walk her home. We walked down Bickler Street to her house, and I carried her books. When we arrived at Susan's front porch, Gramps was a bit shocked to see little Susan, fifteen at the time, bring home a fella from school. I introduced myself, and Gramps barked that I was a very strapping young man.

I could not help but smell a fantastic aroma coming from the kitchen. Fresh fried chicken sizzling in the skillet, along with collard greens, macaroni and cheese, biscuits and gravy, with apple cobbler for dessert. I was sitting in the living room with Susan but had nothing but fried chicken on my brain. As I answered a barrage of questions from, undenounced to him, one of my future in-laws, little Sue could not take her eyes off me.

Mama made the call, "Come and get it."

Stampeding, Bison made less commotion getting to the dinner table than Papa, Gramps, Bill, Sue's older brother, and I did. Once at the table, the caravan of carnivores devoured every delicious morsel of food in minutes. Then, the apple cobbler and homemade peach ice cream were brought in. I leaned slightly toward Sue and asked if she and her family ate like this every evening.

Sue nodded and said, "Yes, doesn't everyone?"

"No, I have watched my mother burn water on an electric stove. I love my mom dearly, but she can't even boil potatoes, and you can play half rubber with her biscuits. They are hard as a rock."

Sue looked puzzled, "Half rubber, what's that?"

"It's sort of like baseball, but two people or more can play. All you need is a broom handle and half a pink rubber ball the size of a baseball or some of my mom's biscuits. If the batter hits the half rubber over the pitcher's head, it counts as a home run. If they hit it on the ground, it's an out. After three outs, the pitcher and the batter switch sides. Usually, it goes for at least nine innings. Some of my teammates and I would play before baseball practice. But, enough about baseball. What do you like to do for fun?"

Sue told me to finish my ice cream and that we would talk after she showed me her archery stuff.

After that incredible meal, Sue and I went outside behind a large garage building, and there were ten large bales of hay. The two in the approximate center had a burlap bag attached to the front, which was painted up to look like a bull's eye. Sue reached into her gunny sack and pulled out an arm guard and a beautiful quiver of arrows. We walked approximately thirty paces from the hay bales. Then Sue proceeded to nock three arrows on her bow and put them two inches apart in the center of the burlap target. I was impressed. I tried and managed to hit the burlap target once in five attempts. However, I soon realized I was much better at baseball than archery.

The sun was starting to fade on that cool, crisp November day. I asked if I could call my mom and dad to come pick me up.

***

The entire ride home I could think of nothing but Sue. She was the prettiest flower in Texas. It is amazing when the love bug finally takes a bite at your heart. We started dating almost immediately. I would show up every Friday afternoon twenty minutes before dinner (on purpose.) Sue's mom should have owned a restaurant. Everything she cooked tasted fantastic. Her mother, Tess, was the best Southern scratch cook I ever met. Meatloaf, brisket, pork chops, seafood, everything was amazing. Her dad, Bill Senior, was a talented cook as well. If Sue cooked half as well as either one, I would do very well to marry her at the first opportunity. So that was what I did. There was one issue, though. Bill and Tess insisted that Sue graduate from High School before we got married. Sue was held back and had to repeat the ninth grade, so I would have to wait three years. We did not actually tie the knot until I was a junior in college. At the time, I thought she was worth the wait.

Navigating a three-year long-distance relationship was not easy. I officially proposed the summer prior to her senior year. Sue and I almost broke up a couple of times because she was dating other high school boys prior to our engagement. She was very attractive with her slender full figure and long flowing auburn hair. She was very popular, especially due to being a year older than most of her classmates. The extra year beyond puberty made her almost irresistible to many of her male suitors. Once her acne completely subsided post-junior year,

3

she was quite a catch. She was always naïve and hesitant about sex, even with protection, but I just wrote that off as a religious thing. I assumed that would change once we were married. I was wrong.

Southern weddings in the 1960's tended to be more spectacle than ceremonies. Her mother and grandmother were about as superstitious as they come. Many odd and sometimes complicated rituals had to take place prior to the actual ceremony. Among them was the post-ceremony ring exchange. The preacher must place the engagement ring on the bride's finger prior to being introduced as Mr. and Mrs. at the reception. The vows were said, and the kiss was lovely. We both got wedding cakes shoved down each other's throats.

The only real hitch to the entire day came when my cousins decided to give our honeymoon vehicle a special tune-up. This consisted of switching around the spark plug wires on the distributor cap. My grandfather was supposed to keep a good eye on the car so that it would be ready for our drive to the Smokey Mountains in North Carolina. I turned the key in the ignition, and the car sounded like a backfiring lawn mower. It took me a good hour to straighten that mess out. Sue was crying almost the whole time I worked on fixing that mess. I swore one day I would get even for that. Three years later, I did.

My cousins Pete and Alan did lots of double dating. I devised a plan to catch both in a midnight skinny dip naked and quite a distance from their clothing. They liked to hang out at a local beer joint near a popular swimming pond. I got a couple of girls I grew up with to lure Alan and Pete to the pond and con them into the water, not knowing that the girls had oversized beach towels waiting for them under rocks at the water's edge. The boys swam out to meet their dates. Then the girls high-tailed it back to shore, wrapped themselves in the beach towels, and yelled, "LIGHTS."

Ten sets of car headlights turned on in unison. Pete and Alan were standing at the shoreline wearing nothing but sarcastic smiles. After a few minutes and several camera shots, I walked toward them with a couple more beach towels. I just said, "GOTCHA." Afterward, we all headed back to the beer joint and had a good laugh about the whole thing. People still tell that story to this day. I believe some of the pictures of those two are still on display in that bar. My partners in the scheme were a couple of local farm girls I hung out with in ninth and tenth grade. Bonnie and Daisy were wild creatures at that age. They were only too willing to help me out after they found out what they did to me on my wedding day. Had I known how disclosing they were going to be about our previous exploits, I probably would not have brought Sue along that night. I told Sue that it was a long time before I met her. She gave me the benefit of the doubt, thank goodness.

Our honeymoon was very special for both of us. Sue was still a virgin on our wedding night, so I had to be very gentle with her. She hadn't even experienced an orgasm before. Right after I gave her one, she hugged me for quite a long time. I didn't quite understand why it was so foreign to her sharing such a physically stimulating experience. Almost a week passed before we had full intercourse. She required a great deal of lubrication. I was able to climax her in the missionary position, which I read was not always easy. We weren't really trying to get pregnant; I just wanted Sue to enjoy the intimacy and physical interaction as much as I did. I know she found me very attractive, and she liked pleasing me. Still there was something not quite right about our amorous moments together. It was as if she was afraid to commit to a pleasurable sexual release. I thought maybe she was in some sort of sexual rut. I got the sense that she was faking her orgasms just to make me feel good about myself. This seemed odd in the fact that I got so much pleasure in watching her come as well.

It was very clear that I was married to a submissive, dutiful wife. I asked her if anything was bothering her. I got the same answer every time: "I'm ok." After a year of hearing that, I finally scheduled an appointment with a sex therapist. I found a female doctor who was highly recommended in the area. During the five sessions we attended, I don't think Sue said twenty words the entire time. Dr. Ames told me that, in her expert opinion, she believed Sue was suffering from schizophrenia and recommended we see a psychiatrist right away. Three psychiatrists later I finally found one that she would at least talk to. The doctor suspected childhood trauma, probably molestation very early on. The recent sexual awareness brought on the psychosis. He said medication may help to alleviate some of the trauma, but it would take lots of therapy to help Sue get past the emotional scarring that took place. Now, what was I supposed to do? It's obvious she was not ready to confront her demons. I didn't want to lose her forever. She was still a very dutiful wife in many aspects of our marriage and an amazing housewife. I just prayed that this sexual issue could be resolved somehow.

A few weeks later I came home, and Sue ran up to me and gave me a very passionate kiss, then announced that we were pregnant. Well, she was anyway. I retorted and told her that was wonderful news. Thinking to myself, 'Oh shit!' This was not good! How screwed up was this kid going to grow up to be. Was it possible that this could be a good thing? It would give her something to focus all her attention on. I didn't know. I just didn't know. I guess we would find out in nine months.

Her psychiatrist was optimistic to a point. He said I could expect good things until the child started school. Once any sign of independence became apparent, there would be a major power struggle between the mother and child. Sue would be extremely smothering and would always see them as vulnerable infants needing constant attention. It could cause severe psychosis as the child reached adolescence and early adulthood.

I returned to the Dr. alone and asked him point blank, "Will Sue need to be institutionalized?"

The doctor said, "Yes, there is a good possibility she will need around-the-clock care. You may have a very tough road ahead."

"What if she got an abortion or had a miscarriage?"

"It could be worse, a lot worse!"

I drove home thinking I was in a unique no-win situation. I would probably have to raise this kid by myself either way. Why was mental illness such a taboo topic? There must be a doctor or a clinic that could help mothers with schizophrenia somewhere.

I found a clinic in Boston that had some experience with mothers who survived childhood sexual exploitation. They recommended a six-month to one-year program consisting of drugs and therapy. No guarantees, a 25% success rate, and $2500 a month. The more I investigated this problem, the more I was simply disgusted by the entire mental health community. I had serious doubts as to whether Sue would ever get any proper mental health care anywhere.

Surprisingly, right now, everything is really good. Even the sex is amazing, and I feel a little guilty about knowing what may be coming after the baby is here. I guess, for now, I will just let it ride. There is a ton of stuff to take care of. The nursery is pretty much done. We have a crib, bassinet, and changing table. All the nursery needs now is the kid. That is still four months away. No pickles and ice cream yet. Sue keeps asking for pistachio nuts and peanut butter. I must stop at least once a week for those items on my way home from work. Work is good. I love my job as a civil engineer. I get to solve problems using math all day.

Right now, I am working on a series of bridges that will be connecting two major highways together in north Georgia. This project will keep me busy until Sue's due date.

***

So, I am walking out the door, and Missy, the receptionist, flags me down and tells me Sue has just been taken to the hospital. I jump in the car and head right over. Dr. Patterson meets me in the waiting room and tells me Sue is doing fine and the baby is stillborn.

I said, "But she is in the third trimester."

"It happens. Usually, caused by an abnormal placenta. Only an autopsy will explain the exact cause of death."

"Doc, Susan suffers from schizophrenia, and I don't think that full disclosure of what has happened is a very good idea."

"Bobby, she is going to have to know what is going on. At this point, she is probably aware that the baby is dead or at least suspects that something is severely wrong. We must tell her everything, no matter how painful and upsetting it will be for her. She must start the grieving process."

I didn't want to think about what was going to unfold. The doctor suggested that we go ahead and induce labor now and remove the fetus. He believed it would be less traumatic later. However, I couldn't possibly see how. My guts were all twisted up inside. My unborn daughter, Kelly Ann, would never be cradled in my arms. I would never get to sing her a lullaby or watch her sleep in her new bassinet. I went to the hospital chapel for a while to sort things out in my head. There were a bunch of things that would happen, not the least of all was making the funeral arrangements.

I went back to Sue's room. She was sound asleep and looked so peaceful, just lying there. As I stood next to the bed, watching her for a lengthy period in complete silence, it was so surreal to me that the little person inside her was no longer alive. I asked myself; 'How could this be?' I could still see the baby bump. How could little Kelly be dead? I started to sob. Sue's nurse walked in and saw me crying. She gave me a tissue. I reached out and hugged her as I cried on her shoulder. She did not pull away and hugged me back. Then she kissed me on the cheek and told me that I needed to be strong for my wife to help her get through this. I stepped back, wiped my eyes with the tissue she gave me, blew my nose, and thanked her for being so kind.

She grabbed my hand and said that sometimes her job required acts of compassion and tenderness. God bless us all. Then she told me the doctor would be in to see us in a few moments to discuss a few things. Then she walked out of the room. Sue started to wake up slowly and asked me if the nurse had come in. I said yes and that the doctor would be in soon to talk to us. Sue started to cry and said, "I'm so sorry I lost the baby."

I grabbed her hand and uttered, "Honey, it's not your fault; this is a very rare occurrence. We have to believe that it is God's will that this child is in heaven waiting for us to join her."

Minutes later, the doctor came in and explained all our options to us. After hearing from him, we agreed to let them start inducing her tomorrow morning. Two days later, we left the hospital together and went home.

Chapter 2: Shattered Peace

Life at home in our two-bedroom apartment was far from normal. Sue was now so manically depressed that she barely ate anything, talked about anything, or went outside. Friends would ask how Sue was getting along. I told them she was still in mourning. This was a lie. Sue was in and out of a catatonic state for most of her waking hours. She would wake up, wash up, make a cup of coffee, take a valium, and lay down on the couch and watch TV all day until I came home. This was her routine for the last four and a half months.

Finally, I had enough. I went and talked to her psychiatrist and asked if she needed to be committed for a while. He agreed and started making the necessary arrangements. Sue was indifferent to the entire process. It took five months of intense therapy, but Sue started to show signs of real progress. I would spend the entire day with her each Saturday. She really started to appreciate all of life's gifts and stopped dwelling on everything that had been taken away from her. It would be another six months before Susan would move back in with me.

I had a companion again, but I noticed she had no desire for sex. I think it was a side effect from the anti-depressants she was taking, though the doctors denied it. They kept telling me to be patient and that her libido would return in time. Undenounced to them, my sexual release came in the form of a co-worker. We started the affair soon after Susan was committed. Valarie was divorced. Her ex-husband Thomas was extremely controlling in every part of what was their six-year marriage. I met Tom once by accident while having dinner with

Valerie. I could tell the man had mommy issues right away. It was obvious our friends-with-benefits relationship became healthier than being with Tom. I cared for Valerie very much, but ultimately, I could not give her the one thing she desperately wanted from me: a marriage proposal. Susan was flawed in many ways; she seemed for a time to be ok with a purely platonic relationship.

Valerie would eventually move on. She found another kind, thoughtful man and married him. I had to find another woman willing to share me with Susan.

I met Kimberly at a company cocktail party. We started talking, and the next thing I knew, we were at her place, tearing one-off. I wasn't exactly proud of what I did with her that night. The sex was great. Turns out she was a traveling secretary for one of my bosses' friends. She lived a very promiscuous lifestyle. I guess thirty-six-year-old men need a one-night stand from time to time.

I had a great deal of remorse over Kimberly. Much more so than I ever did with Valarie. I think the difference was commitment. Val and I could appreciate each other during our intimate moments. We both desperately needed someone to talk to who would listen without exercising pettiness or judgment. We would usually make love to each other for an hour or so, then talk to each other about everything.

Valarie was a gifted musician. She played electric guitar, bass, and banjo. Val was in an all-girl rock-n-roll band in high school. I heard her bang a few chords on an acoustic guitar once. She was very impressive.

Soon after I ended the affair with Valarie, Susan started to become amorous again. I was pleasantly surprised by this sudden interest in sex. Come to find out, she desperately wanted to get pregnant again. Sue told me I could not use a condom. I considered the real possibility of another stillborn. Susan kept insisting we should try for another child. She must have read some books because she would seduce me just about every night until she was pregnant again. Then, we were still hot and heavy until about the third trimester. I didn't mind laying off a bit out of concern for the baby.

Almost eleven weeks later, Sue gave birth to a very healthy boy. We named him Joseph Riley Stockton, after her and my great grandfathers. Sue was a changed woman. Now, she had a full-time job taking care of Joey. Sue wanted to have more children, but I insisted on using a condom. A few years later, against the advice of my doctor, I had a vasectomy. End of discussion.

As Joey started to become more independent, Sue became very agitated with him. It was very apparent that she did not want Joey to grow up. She wanted that little helpless infant who continuously required her attention. As early as the age of four, Joey began to resent Sue for the way she would try to control him all the time. Sue would not let him play unsupervised with other children. The games they played were Sue's idea. She always made the snacks they ate. No candy or ice cream, only baked goods, cookies, pies, tarts, cakes, etc. I could see a very unhealthy relationship forming between her and Joey. When I tried to discuss this fact with her, she would immediately clam up or change the subject.

Sue cried all morning the first day Joey went off to kindergarten. Joey thoroughly enjoyed school. Especially all the new friends he made. I warned Sue not to dominate Joey in front of his friends, but she didn't listen. In the second grade, Joey was earmarked as gifted and talented (high IQ for his age.) At the age of nine, Joey's IQ was higher than Sue's.

That became a problem very quickly. Joey's logic skills soon became king to Susan's. I had suspected this issue would arise; I just didn't expect it before Joey's tenth birthday. Now, there was no way to place the genie back in the bottle. I guess I should have considered the intelligence factor when selecting a wife. Me being an engineer, and Susan is a high school graduate on the five-year plan. In retrospect, that was not very fair to Joey. He would have to grow up with a mom who was schizophrenic and mentally challenged. She would never be able to help him with his homework. I just hope he can forgive her like I have for not being smart. To her credit, she is a wonderful housewife. I guess that is the tradeoff. Honestly, I hadn't expected to discover such a deep-rooted mental instability in my marriage. I should have been more careful. I wasn't aware at the time, but apparently, schizophrenia is common in children of alcoholic parents. It would have been nice to know that piece of information before committing to a very dysfunctional marriage. Almost everything that Susan's psychiatrist told me has come to pass. All the relationship struggles, sexual inhibitions, and bouts of depression have transpired in recent years. I could just say the hell with it: divorce Sue on the grounds of mental incompetency and find a more suitable mother for Joey. That leaves many loose ends.

If I retain full custody of Joey, Sue would be devastated and probably have to be recommitted to an asylum. That would leave lots of explaining for Joey, especially if he pursued any type of career in big government or law enforcement. Then, there is the possibility of Susan becoming depressed to the point of suicide. That would be severely selfish of me to just cast her aside, and my colleagues would recognize what I did. It could really hurt me career-wise. Maybe I would not be chastised for doing it, but it would still be a very shitty thing to do. I will have to find a solution to controlling Sue's mental illness and keep my career on track. Everyone has skeletons, so I'm told. I need to find a good therapist for Sue. I will have to communicate this to Joey.

Joey and I were going on a bass fishing trip very soon. That would be the perfect opportunity to discuss this with him. It was a clear sky at five am when Joey and I left for Lake Rollins. We arrived at the fish camp around 6:30 am. The sun was just peeking over the horizon as I grabbed the oars, slipped them into the cleats, and rowed us out into a patch of giant lily pads. We both baited our hooks with night crawlers and tossed our lines in the calm lake water.

Staring at our red and white bobbers, I said, "Joey, there is something I need to talk to you about, man to man. I realize you are only eleven, soon to be twelve, but this conversation can't wait. It concerns your mom's mental illness." Joey looked over at me, stunned, and did not say a word.

"Son, you probably notice from time to time that your mom seems confused about things."

"Yes, Dad, I do see Mom dazed about things once in a while."

"Well, she suffers from schizophrenia and depression. The medication she takes for it can make her a little spacey at times."

"What is skits o prana?"

"Schizophrenia is a neurological disorder that causes people to become extremely disoriented at times, possibly. They may even see things that aren't there. It can cause people to get very nervous and feel unsafe. Sometimes they will get excited and not be able to control themselves. You and I have seen Mom get like that often when she forgets to take her medication. She goes to a doctor once a week when you are in school. She is slowly getting better."

"Why is Mom like that?"

"Apparently, it is common in children of alcoholics. Her dad drank a lot because of his high-stress job. It seems there is a chemical imbalance that exists in children of alcoholics, causing them to suffer from this disorder. It makes the parents turn to substance abuse, and the kids become schizophrenic. That is all I know. I wish your mom were not like this. It is important that we try to help her as much as possible while facing this ordeal of hers."

"Ok, Dad, I will try to do as much as I can, and I won't tell anybody."

"Please don't tell her or anyone else about this conversation. It could prove very embarrassing for all of us."

"Ok, pop. I won't say anything. Is mom always going to be like that?"

"There is a very good possibility that she will always struggle with mental illness. The good news is if we can convince her to trust the doctors enough to stay on her prescribed medication, she could live a normal life. Suppose she is willing to take her meds. Some of them have side effects that Mom doesn't like."

I started to suspect that Sue may have been hallucinating for some time. I started hearing one-sided conversations while she was alone in the bathroom. I distinctly heard her talking about something. Two weeks later, she had a psychotic episode with Joey. While driving to the grocery store, a police car passed her on the road and turned on its blue lights. The cop drove forward about 500 feet, then turned his lights off. Something snapped in her head because she immediately went home, packed a suitcase, picked Joey up an hour early from school, and headed for the bus terminal.

She was convinced that the police were after her and she had to get out of town by noon. Apparently, she saw the cops' blue light flash twelve times. If Joey had not been able to convince her not to get on the bus, there would be no telling where they may have ended up. Joey pointed out to her that the big clock on the bus station marquee read 1:30 pm. Nothing happened.

Joey told Mom, "You do what you want. I am not getting on that bus."

Then he managed to convince her to drive home and call me at work. I think that might have been the day that Joey's childhood ended. He was six weeks shy of his twelfth birthday. It was not supposed to be like that.

I was ready to file for divorce and throw Sue in an asylum for good. As far as I was concerned, she deserved it. Then I thought of the consequences. My career would take a hit. I probably would never make a partner in my engineering firm. It would be tantamount to career suicide. It could mean lots of retirement savings down the tubes. Even a dysfunctional marriage was better than a divorce. If Joey's friends ever found out, he would be ruined socially and professionally. The next day, I marched Sue back into her shrink's office and told him that we had to find a way to fix this. Sue could end up getting arrested or worse. So, Dr. Brocker prescribed stronger medication to eliminate the psychotic episodes. This made her drowsy. She ended up sleeping twelve to fourteen hours a day.

Chapter 3: A Family on the Edge

"You mean it, Dad? Is grandma really coming to live with us?"

"Yes, Grandma Tess is going to stay with us for a while. She will help us with most of the domestic duties while Mom is adjusting to her new medical treatment. I just hope we can survive all that authentic southern cooking. Grandma cooks everything with butter and bacon grease. Lord, help my waistline."

I have to go pick up Tess at the bus station Tuesday morning. I haven't told her everything about Sue's condition. Well, not about the hallucinations yet. How do you tell your mother-in-law that her daughter is suffering from severe mental illness? She is taking narcotics as part of her treatment. She may need to be institutionalized again, and I hope I can find the right words.

I went to pick up Tess alone from the bus station, and I took her to lunch. We talked for several hours. She was not happy at all when I disclosed the real reason for her visit.

"Look here, Bobby, I don't appreciate being used like this. I love you for thinking of Sue's well-being, but I don't appreciate being lied to, no matter what your motives were. You know me. I am a straight shooter. I don't go in for this secrecy crap! How is little Joey handling all this?"

"Pretty well, considering he was caught in the middle of a psychotic episode last week. That is why you are here. It will take both of us working together, if Sue is to have any chance at normalcy. The drugs she is taking daily keep her sane, but she is exhausted. I need you to help with the meals, laundry, and grocery shopping. Joey and I can help with cleaning up around the house. Sue is very excited to see you. Joey is bouncing off the walls over the fact that you are coming. Just don't feed us fried chicken every night. I won't be able to fit into my work clothes. Those suits are expensive. I can't just go out and buy one every time you make apple cobbler. By the way, you are probably the best southern scratch cook I have ever known, and thank you so much for understanding how delicate this situation is for everyone involved. Unfortunately, the fewer people who are aware of Sue's mental state, the better. Mental illness has such a stigma attached right now that it could hurt me at work and Joey at school. I don't like this secrecy either, but at this point, we don't have a choice."

"Ok, Bobby, I am with you as long as Sue shows progress."

"Fair enough. Now let's order lunch."

***

It is obvious I won't be able to explore any extramarital social interaction with Tess around. I will have to appear the dutiful husband for a while. That will not be difficult since work has been so taxing lately. The one overriding theme of any infidelity is not to get caught. No matter how great the desire, never get caught! Besides, I do love Sue very much, and I am terrified of her mother. Tess is the most intelligent, self-educated woman I have ever met in my life. Tess is an amazing, funny, sweet, gifted, charismatic woman. I am sure she is part of the reason I liked Sue so much. Many of the intriguing qualities that made me fall in love with Sue I see in Tess. I pray that somehow, as a family, we will be able to overcome this mammoth hurdle and have some sense of balance again.

Now, when I leave for work in the morning, I have every confidence in Tess to keep Sue safe from harm, whether self-inflicted or otherwise. It has been three weeks now, and the medication is starting to help. Sue has stopped having paranoid episodes when she is stressed. Again, there is no interest in sex. Maybe when Tess goes back home in a few more weeks, that will change. I have serious doubts, though. Even her therapist is concerned with Sue's lack of sexual interest. She has been going to sessions with and without me for two months now, and she still refuses to discuss anything to do with intimacy. I remain a patient, supportive husband through all this.

Lying beside Sue every night and longing for a simple caress is becoming quite frustrating. I want to run my hands ever so gently along her incredible figure. The scent of her perfume is still intoxicating. Again, I am forced to take a midnight dip in our swimming pool to cool off. Sue hands me a towel as I exit our indoor pool, completely nude.

"Honey, I'm sorry that I can't have sex with you right now. I fantasize about being with you during the day. Then, when you come home, I lose all desire to lie with you and to pleasure you like I used to. I don't even want to discuss it. The medication must be doing this to me."

"I understand sweetheart, but I do find myself wanting to hold you in my arms, to kiss you passionately. I want to make love to all of you, your body and soul together. You are such a beautiful, desirable, stimulating woman. I just want to share deep, arousing physical intimacy with you right now. I need a sex partner. When you are ready, I will be here."

"Thank you for being so patient with me. I appreciate you." Then Sue kissed me on the corner of my mouth and went back upstairs to bed. Just another night in the pool. I don't mind so much the lack of sexual release. It's the intimacy I miss. Even affairs with other women cannot fill that void. There is never enough time to truly savor all the intricate moments that married couples share during sex. I miss Sue's hands clenched with mine in bed while being entangled atop one another. The wet, passionate kisses that stimulate every inch of my body. The foreplay. I miss the slow, methodical foreplay that lovers share. Sue is, or was, great at foreplay.

After my affair with Valarie ended, I realized that my time with her was a gift and a curse. She was a master when it came, no pun intended, to stimulate my erogenous zones. That woman could get me so hot I thought I would pass out. Then I would have this blistering hot orgasm. But the downside was it always ended too soon. A couple of hours together, then a ten-to-fifteen-day separation because I had to be so careful. It was a forty-five-minute drive to our out-of-town destinations. The drive back was the worst. I could tell Val wanted much more than sex from our relationship, but I was never going to be in a position where I would be willing to give up Sue and Joey. As I reminisce, the reality is that it is possible to love two women at the same time while disclosing completely different expectations of individual relationships. I remit a selfish loss in both endeavors. The sexual high that I experienced with Valarie never compensated for the lack of intimacy I lost with Sue. Val was my quick fix, my candy, my forbidden sin. All the while eating away at the heart of my selfish desire to lie with Sue again in guiltless sexual bliss. Sue has given me a happy, healthy, intelligent son to cherish all the remaining days of my life. So be it. I went back upstairs, crawled into bed, kissed Sue on the shoulder, and whispered, "Good night, my sweet darling." Then I rolled over and fell into a soft, warm, satisfying sleep.

This morning, I found Joey waking me up frantically, boasting, "Come on, Dad, the little league tryouts are this morning. You promised to take me."

I beat the sleep out of my eyes, rolled out of bed, and said, "Ok, ok."

I dragged myself in front of the bathroom mirror, turned on the hot water, dragged a razor across my face, rinsed off, got dressed, and ran down to the kitchen. Sue had hot coffee, pancakes, and fresh bacon waiting for me as I flopped into my chair at the table. I sat there for one moment and took in the quaint elegance of my surroundings. I thought to myself, this is going to be a good day. Tess came out of the downstairs bathroom and sat down beside me. Then she announced that her work here was finished. She could no longer be a substantial help to us. So, we agreed that she would hop a bus home on Friday. I gathered from her tone that she got her fill of us for a while. I remained silent and just enjoyed my delicious pancakes. A silent note to self: definitely a good day.

Joey and I arrived at the ballpark for tryouts.

"Okay, son, go out there and knock them dead."

He jumped out of the car and raced to the line where all the other boys were. The tryout consisted of three events. Five attempts to hit, throw, and catch a baseball. Joey went 5 for 5 in each event. Unfortunately, there were 37 other participants who did the same, with only 25 slots open. I don't mind saying I was very nervous that Joey's name would not be called. There must have been 150 kids trying out that day. I suggested another league that was a little less competitive, but Joey would have none of that. It was the travel league or nothing.

In the interim, prior to the results being announced, we grabbed a couple of hot dogs and sodas from the catering truck. Boy, Joey loves ketchup. His dog was drowning in it. Hey, you're only a kid once. Finally, the results were going to be announced. 25 names were called, and Joey's name was not. My heart sank for a time. Then the coach said this year. They are selecting 5 alternates instead of a mid-season trial to fill any short rosters. Joey was the first alternate. A week later, he was on the Valley Kings roster. I had never been so happy. Later, Coach Burns told Joey that 3 kids scored 1 point higher than he did at the trials. That was why the coaches decided to include alternates this year. They wanted to make sure Joey and one other kid named Jimmy eventually made the roster. God I was never so proud about anything in my life. Everybody needs a quality win once and a while.

Tess decided to stay another couple of weeks on the odd chance that she might see Joey play in a game. She got her wish. In the second game, a kid broke his ankle, sliding into second base. That put Joey in the line-up batting ninth the very next game. Any butterflies he had were gone on the second pitch, which he slammed into left-center and stretched it to a double. The following at-bat, he hit a screaming line drive over third base for a single. On the next pitch, he stole second. Joey went 4 for 4 with 3 stolen bases. He did not bat ninth in the next game; hitting fifth, he went 3 for 3 with 2 stolen bases and 1 walk. Later in the season, he ran into better pitching. Joey was batting well over 400 despite the better competition.

Joey's squad made the second round of the playoffs before losing to the eventual league champion. Joey batted 478 with 18 stolen bases that year. The league's stolen base record was 22. Being an alternate cost him two games at the beginning of the season. Who knows, if he played in those games 23 stolen bases may have been possible. In any case, it was an amazing season. I assumed Joey would pursue baseball in high school. I was wrong. He developed a taste for football, and that was the end of his baseball career. That's ok. He was a very good middle linebacker, which allowed him to walk onto a small college roster until he got injured his freshman year.

Chapter 4: The Breaking Point

Monday morning finds me at work on time, as always, unlike some of my less punctual cohorts. Hey, some people just don't put emphasis on that if the work gets done on time. What the hell, we are all on salary anyhow. My secretary informed me that Mr. Britt, the senior partner, needs me in his office right away. So, I topped off my coffee cup and made a beeline to his office.

"Good morning, Mr. Britt."

"Bobby, I need you to go to Broken Mill, Arkansas, immediately; they have a bridge that has a stress fracture problem. I told them I would send my best man right away. Look over the damage and call me immediately. We don't have a helicopter available, so you will have to drive. Use a company car. It's about a three-and-a-half-hour trip. Go ahead and stay the night."

"Yes, sir, I will call you as soon as I inspect the bridge."

"Have a safe trip."

I nodded and headed right out the door, hopped into the company sedan drove to the house to grab a change of clothing and hygiene items, kissed Sue, and I was off to Arkansas. I forgot just how beautiful the Ozarks were in late fall. I wished I could have brought Sue and Joey with me.

Broken Mill was, in my opinion, the original one-horse town, right down to the Civil War statue in the center square. Pristine, quiet and overwhelmingly conservative to a fault. The bridge was not hard to find. It was the only one in the town. I shot a roll of film to document the damage and called Mr. Britt immediately.

"Ok, Bobby, I will see you in a couple of days."

I hung up the cell phone and proceeded to the only film developer in town, Bill's drugstore. Bill was a very nice gentleman. I inquired about lodging for the night. He directed me to Kat's place down the street. Kat's place was impossible to miss. It consisted of a very ornate two-story hotel that was something right out of the 19th century. Once inside, I was blown away by the architecture and ambiance of the place. A gilded Age Museum is hidden in the Ozark mountains. Then I met Katherine. Short auburn hair, piercing brown eyes, the smell of jasmine and wildflowers, and a radiant smile that I found intoxicating.

"How can I help you, sir?"

"I need a room for one night."

"Please fill out the registration card, and I will show you to your room straight away."

"Thank you. How much is the room?"

"A single for one night is $48."

"Excellent."

I followed Kat, as she preferred to be called, up to room number three. Then she told me the bar opened at 4 pm. Dinner was promptly at 6 pm. Family-style local fare. I offered a gratuity, but she graciously exited, closing the door behind her. I stepped out onto the terrace overlooking the creek running through the center of town, sat down in one of the patio chairs, and proceeded to fall asleep immersed in cool

Ozark vespers that seemed to transport me back in time. I was vigorously awakened by the sound and smell of steak sizzling on a grille. I scratched, yawned, and waded back into my room. Then, I made myself presentable enough to go down and eat. I headed for the bar where Kat was pouring drinks. I inquired about the history of the hotel.

"The hotel was built just prior to the Civil War by a local merchant who ended up winning a gold mine in a poker game. A week after he filed a claim on the deed, there was a cave-in at his mine. Nobody was inside at the time. After the repairs were made and all the debris was removed, a pocket of ore was discovered. It yielded over $80,000 before it ran dry. Not one flake of gold has come out of that mine since then. The gold built this hotel."

"Wow, what a great story."

"The last owner, Ezekiel Tate, nephew of Rufus Tate, inherited the hotel and proceeded to run it into bankruptcy. I bought the hotel with a partner at auction, whom I bought out six years ago. It's all mine, bought and paid for. All the furnishings are mid to late 19th century. Nothing has been changed since old man Tate built the place, except the name of course. Kat's Corner is my little corner of the world. I have no family to pass it on, so when I die, this will be donated to the State Historical Society as a living history museum. Would you like me to freshen your drink for you? Enough about me. What's your story, handsome blue-eyed stranger?"

"Ok, my name, as you know, is Bobby, and I am an Engineer. I had to inspect the bridge. I'm married, have one son who just turned twelve, and am gainfully employed, hoping to make partner in the next five years."

"Bobby, you did not say happily married."

"No, I didn't. You are very perceptive."

"It comes with the job. I can freshen up your drink upstairs if you would like?"

"I would like that very much."

We made love for hours. I knew it was only going to be for one night, but it came at a time when I really needed to express myself in physical candor. We walked out onto her terrace, which was markedly larger than the one in my room, sat down, and gazed at the quarter moon.

"Kat, obviously, I am not the first man you have bedded this way."

"No, but I am very selective. I can tell when a man needs to be reminded he is still a man. I have been with dozens of gentlemen, but you, I will think fondly of you for quite some time. You have a quiet, seductive manner and a lovely physical touch, which I find very pleasurable. In case I don't remember to mention it, thank you for a wonderful romantic evening."

"You are very welcome and thank you as well."

"Kat, I would sincerely love to wake up in your arms tomorrow morning, but I fear my heart would pine egregiously for another night like this."

"Ok, but that doesn't mean we cannot tear off another quickie."

"You are incorrigible, okay."

Kat's version of a quickie turned out to be three quickies. She kissed me on the forehead, ran her hand gently across my flaccid, worn-out penis, and exited the room. I was utterly exhausted, but you could not beat the smile off my face with a sledgehammer. I woke up to the sound of the telephone.

I placed the receiver up to my ear, and a man's voice exclaimed, "Courtesy wakeup call."

Then, he abruptly hung up on the other end. I lay in bed staring at the mirrored ceiling, reminiscing. What a night. I cleaned up, dressed, packed up and scurried downstairs, jumped into my car. I turned the key over in the ignition, looked up, and there was Kat standing beside the hood. She walked to my window.

I rolled it down, and she poked her head in and gave me a passionate kiss I will not soon forget and said, "Goodbye, lover." Then she walked back inside. I shall miss her dearly. I don't mind mentioning that Kat pops into my head more often than I like.

Chapter 5: Unraveling Threads

I am back home to Susan and her special kind of normalcy that I have come to accept. My attitude and tolerance of Sue are starting to wear thin, especially when I know that there are women like Katherine who would not hesitate to satisfy my every need. Tempting as it would be to jump ship, as it were, with a more amorous woman, eventually, that relationship would present its own set of unique problems. People, or more to the point, relationships are complex and complicated.

This presents more of an issue for Joey, having to navigate the mature situations that he constantly faces. Last night, there was an altercation between Sue and me that I wish Joey had not been part of. I regret having lost my temper with Sue in front of him. I came home from the office after a stressful day and let my work dictate my demeanor.

Tess returned home less than a week ago. Sue has not been able to function in a domestic capacity since she left. I came home to a household that I considered to be disheveled. Laundry piled up, Sue was in her bathrobe, and dinner had not been planned, much less ready. This had been going on for nearly a week. I confronted her about what she did all day. All she could come up with to say was, "Momma did such a good job with everything around the house; I assumed you didn't want me to do anything." I told her Tess left last week. "She told you that after she left, you would have to start doing housework again."

"Well, yes, she told me that."

"So, why on earth haven't you started cooking and cleaning again? You know we can't afford to eat out every night."

"I know, I know I will have to start cooking for us again."

"When do you think that is going to happen?"

"I don't know when I get around to it, I guess."

"Well, that doesn't tell me very much. I know the medication you are taking makes you a little sleepy. The doctor said that it would start to dissipate in a few days. You haven't been all that tired lately, have you?"

"No."

"Can you see how frustrating this is for me? If you are feeling okay, why don't you do something around the house."

"I could. I just don't want to. I think I would be better off living with momma."

"What about Joey? Are you just going to abandon him as well? He is your son, for Pete's sake. Look, honey, you are going to have to come to grips with your mental illness. If you want to keep our marriage intact, then you are going to have to fight for it. Together, we will find a way to get you through this, but giving up and running home to momma is not the answer. I, we need you to stay and help us become a functional family again."

"Ok, I will try."

At my request, Sue entered the kitchen and prepared a hasty dinner. Prior to her mental episodes, Sue was becoming a very good Southern cook. I so looked forward to her evening meals. She took pride in her cooking. I know she really enjoyed doing things for Joey and me. I had hoped she would find a way to convince herself that the only way to combat her mental instability was to stay home and work things out. Sue called us to the dinner table, and we all sat down. Tuna sandwiches on white bread and ice water. I gazed over to Sue sitting there wearing the nightgown that she wore to bed last night, covered in her burnt orange housecoat. She just sat there piously with her hands folded. I am thinking to myself, we just got groceries two days ago. There was half a meatloaf, and scalloped potatoes left in the fridge from last night. All she had to do was heat it up and steam a vegetable. Sue had to go out of her way to make something this crummy. This was done on purpose. Well, I lost it. I grabbed the pitcher and emptied the contents onto Sue's face, hair, and dirty bathrobe. I said, "There, I threw water at you; now you can go home to momma."

"I will."

Joey was stunned. I don't think he knew how fragile our marriage was until that very moment. I walked into the master bedroom and witnessed Susan packing a suitcase. We got into a devilish argument about her leaving. I know Joey must have heard me yelling at Sue. I wasn't really thinking straight. That dinner was the first time Sue had done anything spiteful toward me. Up to that point, I was able to keep a civil tongue in my head despite all her abnormal behavior. I snapped. Everyone has just so much they can take. I saw that tuna sandwich, and boom! The only good thing that came out of that meal was it finally got Sue talking again. She had to. I don't think she really wanted to go home crying to mom. I told her point blank if she left that night, we were finished. I walked out of the room and headed for the garage. Joey was already there, leaning on the trunk of the car. Joey asked me if Mom was leaving. I told him I did not know, but I hoped she was going to stay.

"Dad, what's wrong with Mom?"

"It's the schizophrenia which is complicated by the manic depression."

"Is the medication helping her at all? I see her taking it when I get home from school."

"Yes, but some of her meds have strong side effects, like the Haldol, for instance. It works to alleviate her psychotic events like the one she had with you. The main side effect is that it can lower her blood pressure. This affects her energy level. Another is Thorazine. It has more side effects. I don't like her being on Thorazine. The doctor told me straight she needed to be on it for a while. Your grandmother had another remedy for her low energy level. She just kept feeding her four to five times a day. I had to put a stop to that."

"Dad, do you remember the time I told Mom I was going to kill myself?"

"Yes, vaguely, what exactly happened?"

"I was playing in the garage with a few of my friends, and Mom opened the garage door. Then she proceeded to ask everyone what was going on. So, I began sobbing and said loudly, "If you don't leave us alone, I will kill myself." I was holding my pocket knife in my right hand at the time. Then I thrust it toward my chest. I don't think Mom realized the blade was not folded open at the time. Then she slammed the door and ran off. Sorry about that. I hope that didn't add to Mom's problems."

"Yes and no, son, that would be just another minute incident that Mom would have trouble deciphering. You and I know that you were speaking metaphorically to get your point across. Who knows what went through your mom's mind that day."

"Can Mom get better?"

"I hope so; individuals diagnosed with schizophrenia usually deal with some level of hysteria for the rest of their lives. That's the ugly truth about mental illness. It never completely goes away. Almost as if it is hiding in some very dark corner somewhere, just waiting to unleash chaos in a person's psyche. I really wish I could make this illness that Mom struggles with go away once and for all. There is no easy answer to this riddle or, in Mom's case, conspiracy brought on by coincidence."

"Oh, like when the cop flashed his lights, and Mom thought we had to get out of town."

"Exactly, she has trouble putting confusing events into logical perspective. It may be a side effect of her learning disability. Mom failed the ninth grade in high school. I told her that she was on the five-year plan same as me. I only took five years to finish my bachelor's in engineering. I worked half a year as a freshman and sophomore. Mom worked, too. She worked in a pizza parlor as a waitress. Apparently, she messed up many orders and ended up getting fired. After that, Mom got hired by a cafeteria, and she did a pretty good job there. The money helped get us through; that was the important thing. Even back then, there were signs of mental illness that I chose to ignore. I was busy trying to get through thermodynamics. I figured it was just the newlywed break-in period. Looking back, I should have taken her to a psychologist right away. Sometimes, I can be stubborn that way.”

“You, Dad, stubborn, perish the thought.”

“No, you’re right. One of my more obvious character flaws is the fact that I never give up on anything, or at least try not to. Sometimes, it’s probably better to cut your losses and live to stand and fight another day. Not me; I will squeeze that wine grape until it fills the bottle. I have to be that way at work. The project always comes first and must come in on time. We better go check on Mom.”

Joey and I found Susan unpacking in the bedroom.

“So, honey, I guess you decided to stay.”

“Yes, I did. You are right, as usual; I just needed a moment to see what was best for me. My place is with you and little Joey.”

“Mom, I am as tall as you are. I’m not so little anymore.”

“Ok, but don’t you be growing up too fast. You’re still my little boy.”

“Aw, Mom!” Then Joey walked out of the room.

“Sue, why do you have to belittle him like that? Very soon, your little boy is going to be a grown man, and he is going to resent the living hell out of you if you carry on like that. So, you better be careful.”

“He’s a long way from being a man.”

“No, he is not, and you better find a way to deal with him becoming less dependent on you. What are you going to do when he goes out on his first date? You can’t go with him. From that point on, you will be the other woman in his life. All I am saying is you need to prepare yourself for when that day comes, and it isn't going to be long. Joey is already showing signs of puberty."

"I have eyes, and I see he is growing." She started to sob. "I just didn't think he would grow up so fast. It's not fair. Just yesterday, he was this beautiful, fragile, adorable little thing I held in my arms, watching him fall asleep. Now he is bigger than I am." I sat down beside Sue on the edge of the bed and handed her a tissue. When she blew her nose, it sounded like a loud dog fart.

"Hey, sweetheart, why don't we all go out and see a drive-in movie? We'll get sodas and a bucket of popcorn. Let's try and lighten the mood a little. I'm sorry I lost my temper earlier. I was frustrated and a little hurt. I apologize."

"Ok, thank you. I would like to go to the movies, too."

I called her bluff, and it worked. I was really worried she was going to run away to her mother. I am relieved that she didn't. Sometimes, I forget how resilient she can be. I just have to give her time to work through things herself. Sue may have made a breakthrough from this episode.

"What do you think doctor?"

"Yes, confronting Susan may have given her the confidence to move on, but you took an awfully big chance going after her the way you did. I realize that you were genuinely pissed off with Sue at the time, but that open egression could have backfired and caused her to shut down even further. I suspect that is how Sue dealt with hurtful situations in the past. There are many disturbing repressed memories trapped inside that woman that eventually need to come out. When they do, both you and Joey must be patient, loving, and supportive of her. In addition, make sure she stays on her medication. Let her psychologist work to alleviate the ugliness in her past."

"Okay, doc."

I left my psychologist's office feeling lucky; I think I dodged a bullet. Well, it worked, so I will say a prayer and see what the next day brings. Sue has become more interested in taking care of the daily chores around the house, and her energy level has increased despite the medication. I am somewhat optimistic going forward that we may resemble a functional family again. Little did I suspect the S curve that was creeping in our direction.

Chapter 6: A Temporary Escape

It was a hot, lazy Friday afternoon in September. I was sitting in my office pretending to look busy before heading home for the weekend. We were planning an overnight trip to the beach. An old college buddy had a beach house. Jimmy T. and his family invited us over for the weekend. I was looking forward to the surf fishing. I would get to throw a line in the water, sit back, and hope the fish let me sleep under my lean-to all afternoon.

On my way out the door, I was summoned into Briggs's office.

"Bobby, I have another assignment for you. I need you to go to Atlanta for a few months with your family, of course."

"A few months?"

"Yes, the new satellite office is opening in three weeks, and I need you to cover for Douglas until his Europe contract is complete, which should be in ten to twelve weeks. Then he will take over. I have a house where you and your family can stay in rent-free. While there you will earn double your regular salary. When you get back your promotion to junior partner will have been approved. As a junior partner, you will receive a ten percent profit share. Approximately 15,000 a year, in addition to your regular salary, is doubled. How does Britt, Douglas, Waters & Stockton sound to you."

"Just fine!"

"Go home and tell your wife the good news."

"Thanks, I will."

I kept shaking Mr. Britt's hand for almost a minute and ran out of the office down into the parking lot, got in my car, and screamed the biggest, "Yahoo!" Then I just sat there and thought I just got a 100% salary increase. Now I can afford that new toothbrush I have been wanting. What the heck, toothbrushes all around. I drove home exercising a great deal of decorum and restraint. I pulled into the driveway and saw Joey engaged in one of his little woodworking projects.

He likes building tall ships from scratch. Most of them are made of balsa wood. Sometimes, I am blown away by some of the materials he uses. His cannons are made from brass .22 shells. It creates a nice effect. The sails are pillow-ticking and hardened with liquid laundry starch. Every time I try to interject some engineering into his project, he throws me to the curb. He tells me it's just art, Dad. I'm not going to sail it across the Atlantic. He's right; I need to let him enjoy the time he has left as an adolescent. Point taken: I do enjoy the aesthetics of his projects when he allows me in his room.

I pulled into the garage, still bubbling over with excitement, but I decided to wait until dinner to give them the good news. Sue made shrimp casserole, a favorite of mine. We usually have seafood on Friday. I waited for the ominous, 'It's ready,' then headed for the table. Sue asked me how my day was, and I exploded with the good news. The joy we shared as a family that night, I will not soon forget.

Sue bombarded me with questions: who, what, when, etc. Joey would have to transfer schools for a short time, but we would be back before Christmas. The firm was paying all our moving expenses. It did not amount to much, mostly clothing.

I could not wait to arrive in Atlanta. The house we stayed in was beautiful. A pristine lawn, indoor swimming pool, game room, three-car garage, and a full liquor cabinet. They must have thrown some outrageous parties here. Everything was perfect. Too perfect.

Three days after we got there, the separation anxiety started to kick in. I was on such an emotional high from the promotion that I neglected to observe how severely Sue had begun to unravel. After a week, she was back in her orange housecoat, watching soap operas all day. The worst part was Joey was front and center during the entire meltdown. I didn't even consider that a two-month hiatus would set Sue off like this. I scrambled to find her a doctor who could be of help. Every psychiatrist and psychologist in the immediate area was booked solid for a month in advance. The best I could come up with was a local clergyman with a minor in sociology. I knew I was asking a lot from that man. After two sessions with Sue, he threw in the towel. He suggested Sue check into a short-term facility that dealt with severe depression. I took her to the only local hospital with a mental health ward. After ten days, she exited the facility well enough to survive the remaining time in Atlanta.

My world was glamorous during the day and hellish at night. It seems odd to say, but Joey kept me grounded during our stay. He was attending a junior high instead of a middle school. Joey learned fast how to survive amongst all those ninth graders. I know he got his first introduction to the female anatomy. He came home from visiting one of the neighbors with his neck and shoulders covered in lipstick. When I asked him about it later, he got all embarrassed, so I knew he had been to first base, maybe second. I felt bad for him. We had to go home in three weeks.

Meanwhile, my love life was non-existent with Susan. I never met a woman who could go hot and cold so fast. The work was great. Job orders were pouring in as fast as we could complete them. Britt was ecstatic with the job I was doing, so no worries there. I just had to make sure that I did not let any part of my home life compromise my work ethic. With eighteen days to go, it looked like I was going to make it.

About a week before we were set to go back home, Joey brought a female guest home for dinner. Cameron was a lovely 13-year-old girl that Joey met at school. She had been very affectionate with Joey. I recognized her lipstick when she walked in. They were an adorable couple. I really hated to see his first taste of puppy love end. Joey took it like a man, though. After we returned home, Joey was quite the ladies' man from then on. I was really impressed with some of the girls he was dating in middle school. They were really cute. My boy was a stud.

Honestly, I think he needed a break from Mom and her hellish mood swings. I was concerned that he might become misogynistic in his social relationships. I called him into the den and closed the door behind him.

"Joey, I am glad to see that you are interested in girls. I feel compelled to mention a few ground rules (as it were) to you. First of all, if you are not aware, you must be respectful at all times when you are out on a date. Never take anything for granted. Also, the easiest way to impress a date is to maintain eye contact and listen intently to the person you are with.

Never disclose anything to your friends after. That is never anybody else's business. Any questions?"

"Well, Dad, lately, it's been just the opposite. Some of my dates are a little too aggressive for me. I just go with it, not to embarrass anyone. Have you ever kissed a girl with really bad breath?"

"No, it sounds like you ran into a girl suffering from halitosis. I never experienced that. I guess I was lucky in that department. I went out with a girl with chronic body odor once. That was a short date. I could barely eat my cheeseburger. I couldn't wait to walk her back home."

"Most of the time, girls just want to put their hand down my pants. They tell me that I am gifted in that department. It is frustrating because they don't always want to finish me off."

"Son, that is something you will have to figure out for yourself. If you feel you are being used, then they are not respecting you. Oh yes, when it comes to male anatomy, for your age, you are gifted in that department. It sounds like your female classmates are discussing your physical attributes with one another."

"Ok, you have given me some things to think about. Thank you, Dad."

That kid might be growing up a little too fast. Damn, I should have told him he should be using a condom.

Joey is thirteen now. I hope he isn't engaging in intercourse yet. I suspect he has already rounded third base and is heading that way. That is a lot of emotional baggage for a young teenager. He should be at least trying to be in a monogamous relationship. Granted, I am not the best role model in that department. All I can really tell him right now is, to be honest with yourself and your partner. Don't let your desires impede your conscience.

Sue does not have any trouble controlling herself when it comes to being amorous. Most of the time that faucet is completely turned off. I have tried doing the dishes often when she is around. I have heard that many women consider that foreplay. Not Sue. It's just another domestic chore she won't have to worry about.

For Joey, it would be two more years, the summer prior to his junior year in high school, before he found a steady girlfriend. Veronica liked to go by her middle name, Carrie. She had middle-length strawberry-blonde hair, was cute as a button, and had a 4.0 GPA. I had hoped some of that would rub off on Joey. He struggled to keep his score above 3.0. They spent oodles of time together, going to sporting events, mostly his football games, dates, school dances, and even study groups. Carrie is a senior and has offers from every university she applied to. Joey is itching to join the Army like his uncle. Unfortunately, he did not return home alive from Vietnam. That war was a complete waste, as most armed conflicts seem to pan out that way. He feels strongly that I should not pay his way through college. Also, Joey has been telling me all along that he is not ready for college yet. I wonder how Carrie feels about his thoughts on that subject. I would assume that she would not be pleased with him.

I was right about Carrie. The minute Joey mentioned going into the military, she left him high and dry. I understand his strong sense of duty, but Carrie had a lot to give up. She really had some strong goals for her life, and she wanted Joey to share them with her. Maybe in the end, it is better they parted ways. It could have turned out similarly to my marriage to Sue. It was obvious that Carrie was smarter than him. He would never accept the role of house husband.

Sue was mortified when Joey told her he wanted to serve in the military right out of high school. All she could imagine was Joey getting killed in a foreign country like her brother. Sue went into one of her manic episodes for a couple of days. Complete with the orange housecoat. That has to be the ugliest housecoat I have ever seen, and she looks like an advertisement for birth control wearing that thing. It is hideous! Joey tried to appease her somewhat by saying he would inquire about a MOS in computers while serving and not volunteer for combat arms. That made her feel a little bit better, but it still didn't get her out of that housecoat.

The three of us sat down together and really discussed all the pros and cons of serving in the military prior to attending college.

"Son, I understand the need to serve others and be part of a solution-based organization. I get all that. But honestly, there are so many other possibilities that don't put you in mortal danger. One compromise would be to join ROTC and go in as an officer. You could do like I did and work for the Corp of Engineers. Granted, I did it as a civilian, but you could work for them as a soldier. Another way would be to get a degree in computing while in ROTC. You would not be in a combat MOS."

"Look, Mom and Dad, this is a decision I need to make on my own."

"Ok, would you consider going to college for one year? If you decide that it is not what you want, then go into the military."

"Alright, but I haven't even applied to any colleges yet. I don't think I can get accepted into a major university. Don't worry about that. Your test scores and GPA are good enough to get you into a small private college. We just need to start applying."

"Ok, Pop, I will give it the old college try."

It wasn't hard to find a small school for Joey. He received several offers to walk on to football programs. Billis College is where he landed. During the first week of practice, Joey broke a bone in his left hand. That was enough to keep him out for the rest of the season. So, a month into his first semester, he dropped out and came home. He couldn't really study on painkillers anyway. Apparently, he suffered a serious injury. He was in a cast for over a month, but after a few weeks of physical therapy, he was good as new. Now, there was nothing to keep Him from enlisting in the Army.

Chapter 7: Between Love and Duty

Joey and I really butted heads when it came to his post-secondary education. The only reason that he went to college at all was to play football and appease me. Joey was still itching to enlist in the Army and finish college after serving in the military. It is a noble and patriotic thing to do, but he is an only child. Sue will be distraught the entire time he is in the service. So, she will probably be torn up over something else whether he enlists or not. It is peacetime now. If that is what he wants and thinks he needs right now, it could be the best thing for him.

Sue called Joey and me downstairs for dinner. She put out a nice spread. Fried catfish, mac-n-cheese, green bean casserole, and rolls. It smelled delicious. I quipped, "Did I forget a birthday? It's not our anniversary."

"No, I just wanted to cook something special for my two men."

"Great, Mom, I can't wait to dig in."

"By the way, Joey, when were you planning to tell your dad and me that you enlisted in the Army."

"I didn't enlist."

"Bullshit, I found your delayed entry paperwork when I went through your dirty clothes!" Sobbing, "Why do you want to die like my brother?"

"Mom, we are not at war right now. Odds are we are going to stay that way."

I intervened, "Listen, son, there are proxy wars starting all over the world. If you choose combat arms, as you told me, you will see action at some point if you stay in long enough."

"Combat! You told me about computers! What the hell were you thinking?"

"Calm down, honey. So, this is a done deal. Can you change your mind?"

"I wouldn't want to even if I could."

Sue ran upstairs crying. Joey walked out the front door. I walked to the kitchen, grabbed a beer out of the fridge, and sat back down at the table. I was not about to let this incredible meal go to waste. A few minutes later, Sue came downstairs and joined me at the table. We both sat and ate in silence. After dinner I put my plate in the dishwasher and started putting the leftovers in the fridge. Sue told me not to worry about them. She would take care of them in a minute. I thanked her and went out to the patio, got undressed, and slipped into the pool. Ten minutes later, Sue stood at the edge of the pool, undressed, and stepped into the water. She swam toward me, wrapped arms and legs around me, and whispered, "Make love to me." I did what she said for fear that she might change her mind. She did not change her mind. However, it would be over a year before she wanted to have sex again. Even her therapist could not explain this strange sexual behavior. He told me to just go with it.

Joey stayed with a friend that night. When he returned that morning, we had a long, serious talk about trust and devotion to family.

"Joey, you are an only child. I am an only child, and my mother is an only child. We have a very small family tree. Mom is completely distraught every time someone in the family dies. When your mom's dad died a few years ago, she was devastated. It took her months to let go. Even now, she cries at the mention of Papa. I just hope you know what you are doing. The military is a dangerous life. Not just the possibility of going into combat. The life expectancy of a soldier in combat is calculated in minutes. Promise me you won't get caught up in all the glory hype."

"Okay, Pop."

So, what's the first thing he does out of basics? He volunteers for a special assignment in Korea. I don't know who was more upset, Sue or me. That was eleven months of absolute hell with Sue while Joey was overseas. She wrote to him every day and called once a week. As an armor crewman, he was constantly out on maneuvers. We met Joey when his plane landed in California. The three of us flew back home together. Joey was on leave for a month before reporting to Colorado. I was impressed when I saw him get off that plane, 6' 3", 240lbs, and chiseled like a Greek statue. He ran the mile in five and a half minutes. I got dizzy watching him. I stopped counting after 25 chin-ups. I did my usual two and took a break. Every woman in the gym was drooling and salivating when he walked by. He collected nine phone numbers and two marriage proposals. Now he is a real stud.

His phone never stopped ringing the entire month he was on leave. Girls and more girls kept calling. Well, maybe not the entire time he was home. Just about every night, women would pick him up at the house. Most nights, he came in before midnight, but not always. He had a few walks of shame or, more to the point, drop-offs of shame early in the morning. Sue didn't care one way or the other. Her little Joey was home. It's like a light switch goes on and off when he comes home and eventually leaves. The minute that Joey rolls out of the driveway, Sue breaks down and cries all day and night. She has to double up on her meds to get over it. Joey spent two years in Colorado Springs before rotating through Germany for eighteen months. I was extremely happy that the newly promoted Sgt. Stockton was due to muster out of the Army.

Joey was supposed to come home in nine days. Then Kuwait was invaded. Unbeknownst to Sue and me, Joey had applied and been accepted to Green Beret School. He was going to go there as a reservist. But with the Kuwait thing, his enlistment was extended. No leaves or passes, the entire armed forces were on alert. I hated to admit it, but Joey looked damn good wearing that Green Beret. His first assignment was in Baghdad, of course, a lot of mop-up duty. My son was destined to be a career soldier. The sooner that I came to grips with that, the better; now, all I had to do was keep Sue on her medication. She was up to twice a day now. She was coming apart at the seams. I wasn't exactly keeping it together all that well. With all this going on and work busier than ever, I put in for a ninety-day leave of absence just to get my head together. I packed up Sue and headed for the coast. I really needed to evaluate what I wanted to do with the rest of my life. I am almost fifty years old with several million dollars in assets. I could retire and just do consulting work until I draw social security. Then, I would only have to worry about Joey and Sue. Twenty-three years in a high-stress job is long enough. Maybe I would sneak a trip back to Broken Mill.

The following Monday morning, I went to work early and waited for my boss to arrive. He was usually the first one in the office, followed by his secretary. Britt walked into the office and saw me waiting for him in the lobby.

"Hello Phillip, how are you this morning."

"I'm fine. Why are you here today?"

"I would like to resign my position as partner in the firm and retire."

"Bobby, I assume that you thought the matter through, and you are not doing this on a whim. That being said, I will submit your resignation to the board on Thursday. Do you mind telling me why you chose to retire at the age of forty-nine?"

"Sure." Then I laid it all out to him going back to the Atlanta trip. He knew about Joey becoming a career soldier but had no clue about Sue's constant struggle with mental illness."

"Look, buddy, you go retire and live the rest of your time on earth the way that you see fit. It sounds like you have several things on your plate right now."

"Thank you for understanding, and as soon as I get my family life in some sort of working order, I would like to consult on a few projects, possibly. That is if you need help with anything later."

"Bobby, I would appreciate that. Please let me know when you are ready to work again. Now go home and unwind yourself for a while."

"I will do that, and thank you for everything." I went back to my desk, gathered up all my junk, and ran out the front door. I loaded everything in the car and sat behind the wheel, staring out into space. Now, what the hell do I do? I am dying for some pancakes. It's almost 9 am, I am headed to my friend Billy's diner for flapjacks and bacon. I pulled into the parking lot, parked, and walked inside. Billy yelled from the kitchen, "Sit down, my friend. Are you having the usual?"

"Yes, pancakes, bacon, and coffee with cream." Billy was an old tennis buddy of mine and my doubles partner for the last ten years. We shared our entire lives together. Billy was privy to all the bad stuff pertaining to Sue. He brought me my breakfast and sat down with me.

"How is Susan doing?"

"About the same, as anxious as ever worrying about Joey. He is a Green Beret now. That is quite an accomplishment for anyone. He can really think on his feet."

"We are still playing doubles tomorrow night, right?"

"Oh yes, I need a break from Sue. I hate saying it that way, but that is how I feel all the time now. She stresses over everything. When to get up in the morning, what to have for breakfast, etc. By the way, this morning I handed in my resignation at work. I am thinking of purchasing a boat. You have a boat guy for your boat, right."

"Yes, Peter Barnes keeps my boat running great. His shop is over on Main Street. I will get you his number. What kind of vessel were you thinking of."

"Nothing like that cabin cruiser you have. I just want a center console skiff, sixteen to eighteen feet. You know, a good dependable fishing boat for about twenty-five to thirty grand. Something Sue and I can go caroming around the marshes with. I love going after Redfish, Blues, Tarpon, etc."

"Definitely go talk to Peter; he can set you up with everything you need. I have to ask. Why did you decide to resign? I'm guessing it was because of Susan. You're still young. Most forty-nine-year-old men don't go around quitting their jobs. They have midlife crises and get it out of their system. With your portfolio, you may be shorting yourself a few million dollars."

"Look, moneybags, I don't own half a dozen businesses like you do, but thanks to you, I am more than sufficiently solvent for early retirement. Piggybacking some of your investments has yielded some fantastic returns. Don't concern yourself about that. Your financial advice has been extremely beneficial over the years. I sincerely thank you for everything."

"You're welcome, my friend." After I devoured that delicious breakfast, Billy and I sat together over coffee for quite a bit. Billy is an amazing guy. At a very young age, his passions and talents melded together. After two years of culinary school and five years working as a sous chef in Chicago, he was ready to go out on his own. He and I were very lucky to see our careers blossom at such an early age. Billy started with two catering trucks, and now he owns six restaurants plus a bakery. That's only half his wealth. The rest came from separate investments. He was born to make money. I am fortunate that some of that gift for profitable investing rubbed off on me. Billy let me in on several very successful business ventures. I was blessed that he let me start out as a silent partner. Billy is a good egg. He believes in giving back to the community; I have seen him donate thousands of turkeys to holiday charities every year. People ask him to run for town council, but he respectfully declines. Billy told me many years ago that wealth and politics don't mix. He has a point.

I have heard wealthy politicians whom I play tennis with retort; they are able to get more things done because their status is above the average working man. True, they may have an easier time in a bad economy, but unless they are self-made, the likelihood of knowing what a pregnant single mother goes through deciding whether to buy groceries or pay the electric bill at the end of the month is scarce. Can he advise a young father how to tell his wife and children that he just got laid off from his job. Billy is right. Politicians should all be self-made individuals. Then maybe they would understand what it is to struggle and sacrifice for others. Local politics is nothing but securing the public safety and fiscal prosperity of the community they work for. That's all, it can't be easy. I know I don't want the job.

Now I am off to see Billy's friend to buy a boat. I drove to Peter Barnes' boat shop and started looking around in the yard. I thought to myself, Bobby you are retired, you are done with the rat race. Now, you get to chase the rats all over the Gulf of Mexico.

No more Bobby, I need this done yesterday. It's a good feeling. This is the first day of the rest of my journey on this earth. I am going to let all of my senses savor every moment going forward from now on. A very pleasant fellow walked up to me and introduced himself as Peter. "Are you Billy's friend Bobby?"

"Yes, I am."

"Follow me, I have something for you." I followed Peter back around the building I parked in front of, and as I passed the back corner of the building, there was an eighteen-foot center console skiff with a red ribboned banner on it that read: **Happy Retirement Bobby.**

Then Peter handed me the keys and said, "It's all yours, compliments of your good friend Billy." I had to use a hankie to compose myself. Billy must have called Peter when he went back to the kitchen while I was finishing my breakfast. That little sneak. I told Peter it was just what I wanted. Peter said, "You are not the only one he's done this type of thing for. Last year, he bought my wife and me a vacation to Hawaii for our tenth wedding anniversary. Billy does this kind of thing all the time. Well, what do you think?"

"What do I think? It's beautiful. I am almost speechless. I don't even have a trailer hitch on my vehicle yet."

"If you have an hour to kill, I can take care of that for you. That will be my retirement gift to you."

I am sitting in Peter's showroom, trying to get a handle on the situation. People don't just walk into a boat dealership and drive one off the lot for free. Unless, apparently, they are friends with Billy and Peter. Except for Joey's birth, this may be the best day of my life. I am going to be selfish and savor this moment for quite some time. To this point in my life, there have been lots of bad days. Too many to mention without beer and alcohol present. Susan has been the bane of my existence for over thirty years. I have never given up on her. That has never been an option, and I understand my role in her life.

Going forward, I will always be a kept man. Kept in a marriage that has very little joy at times.

Susan does not allow herself to find joy in life. The chemical imbalance caused by schizophrenia puts her brain on alert for disruptions of any kind. A burnt bagel in the toaster. A neighbor's dog won't stop barking. Even simple, vague disturbances, which most people choose to ignore, will put Susan in a panic. I watched her burst into tears because she overfilled the automatic drip coffee maker. Most people just yell, "Aw shit!" and clean up the mess. It took me twenty minutes to convince her that it wasn't a punishment from God for drinking too much coffee. We probably do drink too much coffee, but I don't remember reading that in the Ten Commandments. Maybe that was number eleven. Thou shalt monitor one's caffeine intake. I just have not had very many things to celebrate in my life. Work was my escape. While there, I would be hyper-focused on getting the project done on time. My team and I had over a ninety percent success rate, which, considering the industry, was phenomenal. Now, I am afraid I won't have enough distractions in my life to keep me grounded when I must deal with Sue. If I start to regret keeping Sue in my life, I may become angry like before.

I can't let her unfortunate illness push me to a very bad place. I really don't want to become dependent on mood relaxers. Then Joey will have two catatonic seniors to deal with. One is bad enough. Right now, I am in good health, but I need to make some preparations for the possibility that I may die before Susan. Joey would be in a world of hurt if he was not ready to deal with Mom and her special interpretation of life.

Chapter 8: Joey's Awakening

It's fall, and the leaves are falling everywhere. I can't help reminiscing back to when little Joey would jump right into the middle of my raked leaf piles. He knew that aggravated the hell out of me, but he did it anyway. I wish I could watch him do it all over again. Instead, I worry constantly about how he is doing or even what he is doing. I don't think that soldiers realize the constant worry that they put their families through. I got my new boat home, okay? I must say it is a much-needed distraction. Getting out on the water allows me to escape from almost everything. Even Sue likes going out on the boat. I keep losing rods, though. I like to have two lines out for both Sue and I. Invariably if I don't keep a very watchful eye on all four rods, something big will come along and yank one of the rods right out of the rod holder. Then Sue and I watch the rod sink to the bottom of the ocean floor or skip along the surface attached to something really big like a shark or bluefish. Pound for pound Bluefish have got to be the hardest-fighting fish in the ocean. If something big gets on Sues's line, she hands the rod to me, and I get to do all the heavy lifting, landing it in the boat. Then I give the pole back to Sue and snap a photo. Fishing with Sue is never boring.

After five or six hours on the water, we head back to the Marina and call it a day. Marinas are nice; the guys will even clean our catch for us if we give them a gratuity and a couple of filets to take home. I do love freshly caught fish. Many times, we will stop for a meal on the way home. All in all, fishing with Sue can be very relaxing for both of us. Her life seems less stressful when she is out on the water. Although, the weather has to be almost perfect. If it is windy or rainy, she can get a little upset. If a storm cloud rolls in and we see lightning, that's the kiss of death for that trip on the water. It's back to the marina and straight to the restaurant. She is right; being out on the ocean in a small boat during a lightning storm is never a good idea. Between tennis league twice a week and fishing one to two times a week, I stay pretty busy. I wish that I could say that Sue and I didn't find time to worry about Joey being stationed overseas, but we do. I hate to admit it, but I worry almost as much as she does. Well, that's not exactly true; she does the bulk of the worrying for both of us. When I start to get all paranoid about him doing the job that he loves, I think back to a recent conversation we had.

He said, "Pop, I don't want you to concern yourself about me when I am on a mission, and I will tell you why. As a Green Beret, I am one of the best at what I do. Honestly, when it comes right down to it, I am not that easy to kill. I am part of a team; we fight together, we live together, and we do everything together. There is only one thing that we don't do. We never let each other down."

That said, I was still jumping for joy when he called Sue and me to tell us he was coming home on leave. His unit was reporting to Alaska for extreme cold weather training in forty days. That meant that Joey would be staying with us for about four weeks. Sue was bubbling over in anticipation of this event. I never saw her so excited. She cleaned every room in the house at least twice and incinerated every piece of dust with a handheld propane torch.

Joey arrived home right on time, gotta love that military punctuality. We were three again. It felt so good to have little Joey home again, all six foot-four inches of him. Sue was cooking, cleaning, and doing laundry again. She even kissed me in the mouth before bedtime. Around here, that is the same thing as a conjugal visit. I counted myself lucky, rolled over, and went to sleep. The next morning, Joey and I went to the gym for a workout. I was tired just watching him, along with every other woman in the facility. After our workout, we sat down in the lounge at the gym and ordered some lunch. It gave us a chance to get caught up in each other's lives.

"Pop, I met somebody in Colorado several months back. Her name is Rachel. We had been seeing each other quite a bit prior to Kuwait. She is sweet and very smart. I love what I do in the army and I'm not ready to give that up. I had hoped to finish my twenty and then settle down with someone. I am considering getting out of the service for good and devoting myself to her. I have seen way too many service marriages end up in divorce over infidelity, separation anxiety, PTSD, whatever. I know for sure my army career and marriage don't mix."

"You will get no argument from me there. Marriage is difficult enough when the couple is together. I can't fathom a military one. Just look at your mom and I. I hate to admit it to you, but the only reason that I stay married to her is that she would have no one else to take care of her and no place else to go. It would only be a matter of time before she would end up in an asylum permanently. As much as I would like to have an easier way of life, I would always hate myself for abandoning the first and only true love I ever had. I could tell you what I would do in your situation, but it would be based on my interpretation of what's going on in your head. I would be trying to decipher your perception or what I think your goals are right now. Not a chance, kiddo. This is one thing you have to figure out for yourself. I will tell you this much. This decision that you are about to make is going to impact not only you but many others around you. Do not step into your decision haphazardly, or you will regret it. And, oh yes, you will have regrets. Do I have regrets about choosing to stay with your mom all these years? You better believe it. I probably chose the more difficult way, given her medical concerns, but quitting Sue and condemning her to a life of mental incarceration at some level would have eaten me up inside. So, I chose what was best for Mom, and in doing so, allowed you the freedom to live the life that you wanted to. I chose to take care of the people I loved most in the best way that I knew how. Now, my handsome, dutiful son, it is time for you to choose."

"Gee, thanks, pop, I think. Now I am more confused than when I asked you about it."

"Don't worry, son. You will know which way to go when the time comes. So, what is Rachael like? Give me the 411."

"She is beautiful. Smart, sexy, and so alive with a desire to succeed in life. She is a veterinarian. Eventually, she wants to start her own clinic. We went hiking for three days near Boulder last summer. We made love under the stars. It was amazing. I didn't think I could feel this way about anyone."

"I know, it's amazing when the love bug takes a big chunk out of you. I've been there too, with your mom when we were a lot younger. How does she feel about your career in the army?"

"That's where we butt heads. I really want to stay in, but she is ready to take her career to the next level and start her own clinic. It would be a satellite office for the group she currently works for."

"What about your army career?"

"Oh man, my company and Battalion commanders want to send me to Officer Candidate School. They are really pushing me hard. I would love to go. So, you see my dilemma: become an officer or get married and start another career."

"Weigh your pros and cons on both and make the best decision you can. Just remember to be true to yourself because any regrets you have will be no one else's but yours to bear. Honestly, either decision could make you a success. Maybe let your conscience pick this one. For what it's worth, your mom would pick the girl over the army."

"Yes, that is true. I have to tell you, pop, I'm leaning toward OCS right now. My profession is dangerous, but relationships are like the ocean: unpredictable and always demanding your full and undivided attention. It's like choosing the lesser of two evils."

Our food arrived just in time. The conversation was getting overly tense anyway. I told Joey I had retired early because the rat race was starting to get to me. I told him that the three of us could go fishing the next morning. He was very excited to go. I told him everything was biting now, and the weather would be excellent all day tomorrow. So, we headed back home.

Sue was completely beside herself having her little boy home again. I was not looking forward to him leaving for Alaska. That would be a very emotional day for her.

Three weeks passed by way too quickly for me. I woke up, and Joey was gone again, off to the frozen wilderness of our forty-ninth state. I don't know where or how long his training will last. I just know I miss him already. I am so proud of that boy; who am I kidding? He is twice the man I hope to become someday.

I rambled downstairs and polished off a bowl of cereal before I hitched up the boat trailer and headed for the coast. I made the seventy-minute drive just in time to observe the sunrise. I lowered my boat into the water, unhitched the line, and tossed the monkey's fist onto the dock immediately to my left. I parked the trailer and proceeded to the boat. It is crisp and calm. The boat cut right through the glass-like water en route to my first waypoint. Once there, I dropped anchor, cast out a baited line, clipped the bail, and reeled up the slack until the bait was approximately eighteen inches off the bottom. Then I sat back in my chair, placed my rod in the rod holder, popped the top off an ice-cold beer, and just meditated awhile. I secretly thought to myself, I hope the fish don't bother me for a while. This moment is something I would like to savor for more than just one minute. In fact, how about several minutes? I never had days like this working as an engineer. Having to constantly put out Britt's little fires every day. Don't get me wrong. I was happy to be able to work at something that I was passionate about for so many years. If I had not had to deal with Sue's mental health issues, I might still be working there, building more wealth. I guess I am very fortunate to be sitting in a new boat with close to four million dollars in the bank. I worked really hard for over twenty years to secure a nice retirement for myself and my family. Turns out Joey has done very well investing. Over half of his income is already invested. He is still living comfortably on the pay he received as a private. Now, he is a Staff Sergeant. Joey is under thirty with over $100,000 in the bank. Most of it is govt. Bonds. Not too shabby. He could retire around forty with a quarter of a million dollars in the bank. Maybe I will hit him up for a loan when he retires. I hope he gives me a break on the interest rate.

Sue, however, is a real problem right now. Her medication is still presenting several side effects, not the least of which is a stagnant sex drive. Whatever, I'm sure I will get laid again at least once before I die. I could drop a booty call on any of Britt's secretaries any day of the week, but it would be way too risky. I would love to call on Kat again.

Sometimes, I think every man on earth eventually has the opportunity to love and procreate with a woman during their lifetime. I also believe for some, or possibly most, that may or may not be the same woman. That raises a very interesting debate about monogamy. Legally, in the U. S., a man may only be married to one woman at a time. That would be fine as long as the love of your life is also the mother of your children. Couples who choose to have and raise children do so out of love for them. They sacrifice part of their intimacy for the sake of their offspring. They could possibly rekindle the romantic torch again as empty nesters as long as their relationship hasn't grown stale because of the lack of sexual contact. For myself, I feel more like a roommate with Sue than a husband. Financially, we are espoused, but socially, we are roommates.

There was a time when I believed that Sue would be the mother of my children and the love of my life. Now, I find myself trying to justify my actions with other women. I know it is a sin before God. Morally, it is wrong to stray from the marriage bed. But is it? When a man is married to a woman who can't find the means to exercise in conjugal partnership with her spouse, what is the husband to do? Abstain, file for divorce, or lay with another woman. None of these options present a positive outcome.

Abstaining leads to resentfulness and frustration. The frustration could lead to undue stress and hypertension. Divorce can get very ugly when children are involved, even if they are adults. Infidelity can lead to a host of social taboos, trust issues, abandonment issues, etc. The only solution I see is infidelity without getting caught. Then only the man has to find a way to hide his guilt, instead of destroying the rest of what is functioning around him at the time. A combination of abstinence and infidelity may be immoral but practical. The misogynist golden rule is to never, never get caught. When a man is caught, everything the man cares for is put in jeopardy. I have to determine for myself if it is worth it.

Just then, my reel starts singing really loud. I have something big on the line. I grab the rod, set the hook, and sit back for a long fight. It could be a grouper, shark, sting ray, blue, or red; I won't know until I get it to the surface. I have the head turned, but it is slow going. Whatever it is, I hope it's good eating. Foot by foot, I reel in the line, waiting for something to indicate what it is on my hook. Now, my line is swaying back and forth from bow to stern. This big fish is getting close to the surface now. The tail just broke the surface.

A grouper! My heart started pounding. I need to land this big guy. Finally, the head breaks the surface. He is definitely a keeper. I drop my gaff and hoist this monster up over the side and onto the floor of my boat. He measured forty-one inches. That is the biggest fish yet. He barely fit into my live well. I grabbed two ice-cold bottled waters out of my cooler, sat back down, and poured one of them right on top of my head. It was getting up over eighty degrees with no wind, so the water felt very refreshing. Well, that takes care of dinner for several days. I baited my hook again and dropped in almost the same spot. If I don't get another bite today, I will still consider myself very fortunate. A few minutes later, my rod was bent again. This time, it was a nice snapper. He was just below the limit, so I threw him back. This has been a good fishing spot for me lately. I ended the day with 3 grunts, 2 snappers, the big grouper, and 1 big stingray that I threw back. A nice day of catching fish.

Sue was impressed when I got home, especially the size of the Grouper. I had planned to go out again with my friend Allen next week, but Sue insisted I take her the day after tomorrow. I was like, okay, sweetheart, weather permitting, we will head out Friday morning. I ask Sue every night before I go fishing if she wants to come with me. Sometimes she says yes. This is the first time she has asked to join me. I hope she reels in her own fish this time.

Chapter 9: The Weight of Secrets

We hadn't heard from Joey in a few weeks since he arrived in Alaska. I figured it was just his rigorous training schedule. Sue was concerned, but that was nothing new. If she wasn't concerned, then I would have something to worry about. After breakfast, I went out to the shed and got a bag of pool shocks to balance the PH in the swimming pool. I came back in, and someone rang the doorbell.

I yelled from the patio, "Hey honey, can you get that? I am on the patio."

"Ok, I will answer the door." A few minutes later, I started hooking up the automatic scrubber for the pool when I saw Sue walking slowly through the patio door, staring intently at a telegram. Sobbing uncontrollably, she fell back into a patio chair and said, "Joey is missing in Alaska. There was an Avalanche at his training site, and he's still missing."

Now she is screaming, wailing, flailing her arms. I ran over and grabbed her, and tried to wrestle her back to the chair. "Honey, calm down. Stop thrashing about. Look. You said he's missing, not dead. Let's try and get a handle on this. We don't know enough to automatically assume the worst." I took my T-shirt off and let her dry off her face with it. "Here, let me get you something to drink; how about a glass of sherry?"

"Ok." I went into the kitchen and poured a glass of sherry, then headed back toward the patio. I heard the bedroom door close upstairs. I left the sherry on the patio and headed upstairs. The bedroom door was locked. I could hear Sue starting to sob uncontrollably again. I called out to her to open the door, but nothing happened. I backed up a good twenty feet and crashed through the door. There was Sue, clutching a bottle of pills, sitting on the edge of the bed.

"How many did you take? How many!" She fell over on her side, and the remaining pills spilled out on the bed. I grabbed the bottle and read the contents (30 pills.) There were nine left scattered on the bed. I picked up this bottle three days ago. She took eighteen. I grabbed her, put her over my shoulder, and headed downstairs to the garage. I loaded Sue in the car, snapped her seatbelt, ran around, jumped in, pressed the button to open the garage door, hit the ignition, slammed the car into reverse, laid down a donut, and peeled out of the driveway. Enroute to the ER, I called her doctor and told him Sue had just consumed eighteen valiums less than five minutes ago, and we were on our way to the hospital. I hung up with the doc and kept driving.

I pulled up to the ER, and a team was waiting for Sue at the entrance. I parked the car and ran in. Sue's psychiatrist, Dr. Rains, caught me at the door and said, "Wow, big fella, they are pumping her stomach now. You did well. Valium takes a few minutes to take effect. She may feel like crap for a few hours, but you got her here in time. Relax, okay."

"I'm good, she is going to be okay, right."

"Yes, you got her here in about ten minutes. Most of the valium should be in her stomach. You did real good, partner. Now, how's about telling me how she got this way."

"We were just notified that Joey is missing in Alaska. Shit, Joey," I started to sob. "He's missing; there was an avalanche."

"Bobby, he's special forces, right?"

"Yes."

"If anyone could survive one of those, he could. Have a little faith, brother."

About an hour later, an ER staffer came out and told us Sue was out of danger. They were going to keep her here for a couple of days, but she should be okay. I thought to myself, she should be okay, except for the fact that she tried to kill herself. He left that little tidbit out.

Dr. Rains pulled me aside and offered his professional services to me. He told me that I really needed to talk to someone about everything that I am going through right now. It wasn't hard to convince myself that he was right. Three days later, I went to see him. Sue was still in the hospital after a week. Dr. Rains was now recommending Sue be admitted to an Asylum. Her condition is deteriorating fast. Apparently, it will be the best place for her. The doc is really concerned Sue will make another suicide attempt. I reluctantly agreed.

Home is a very lonely place for me now. I drink too much. I am smart enough to know that is not going to solve anything for me. The doctor sent me to a psychologist. She is really good at talking to people. I am old school when it comes to mental therapy. I am a pull yourself up by your bootstraps kind of guy, only I have way too many bootstraps in front of me right now. So, having someone to talk to is a good thing right now.

I decided to take a swim and relax a bit. I got out of the pool and headed to the kitchen for a drink. I checked my messages. Sue, no change in her condition. What, Joey's alive. I called the number immediately. On the other end of the line, I heard, "Hello. Dad, is that you?"

Sobbing and whimpering, I said, "Yes, it's me, son. What? How?"

"Relax Dad, I broke my right leg in two places, and I lost two toes from frostbite, but I am alive and kicking. They offered me a full medical discharge, and I accepted it. What's left of me is coming home. How are you and Mom doing during this ordeal?"

"Mom is in an asylum right now. She tried to commit suicide minutes after we found out you were missing by attempting to swallow an entire bottle of valium. Luckily, I got her to the ER in time to pump her stomach. We were lucky. Your mom went straight to the Asylum from the hospital. Sue is in a catatonic state all the time. She could break out of it any time. That's what the doctors keep telling me. Your grandma Tess is coming to see Mom this weekend. Needless to say, she is not very happy to see me right now. She expects me to divorce your mom and move on with my life. I am not going to give up on your mom. I don't think this is the end for Sue. I have been going to therapy ever since this mess started. How long until you are home."

"A few weeks, I will be able to manage on crutches by then. Mom really lost it, huh? She will recover, right?"

"Eventually, but it's going to be a long road. You coming home will be the best medicine for her. So, you are really getting out for good?"

"Yes, full medical, 100% disability. That combined with my savings, which is now over 125K. I am in great fiscal shape.

Nothing to worry about in that department. Also, I plan to return to school. My fighting days are officially over."

"I am very relieved to hear you say that, son. It is a big load off my shoulders. With your mom in the condition she is in right now, I am in desperate need of a friend right now."

"Pop, you know I will always be there for you. You can call me any time. My day consists of an hour of physical therapy at 8 am and again at 3 pm. The rest of the day I am at my leisure. Lots of cards and chess. My chess game has improved immensely."

"I will do that, son. Would you like me to fly up and accompany you home?"

"That isn't necessary, but I would love it if you would pick me up at the Denver airport. I requested a plane ticket there. I had a notion to return to Colorado Springs and try to see Rachel again if she would talk to me. I have to try and apologize for the way we left things. She was right; it was time to get on with my life. I just hope it's not too late, and she has found someone else."

"There is only one way to find out, and I will be glad to escort you to Colorado Springs. Just let me know when and where."

"Sure, Dad, thanks."

Those weeks prior to Joey arriving in Denver passed by quickly. I was so excited to see him. I am so proud of him for what he has achieved. I feel blessed that he wants me in his life right now. It was never that way with my father.

Chapter 10: When the Past Returns

My daddy was not a kind man. There, I said it for all to hear, except for the fact that I am alone now. It makes no difference; anyone who knew him would characterize Dad as a frustrated product of the times he lived in. Darby William Stockton was a very misunderstood man. I loved him and hated him at the same time. My mother, Anna, was a very understanding woman. Growing up as an only child was not easy due to my father's strict nature. As an adolescent I was expected to be seen and not heard, no exceptions. I was expected to complete my farm chores, which could be intense at times, hauling five-gallon buckets of water for the livestock and milking the cows every morning before school. It gave me a great pitching arm until we bought a milking machine. After that, every pitcher I faced after that used me for batting practice. That's why I became an engineer.

Father and I had very little in common besides the fact that we both adored my mom very much. Daddy just didn't like to talk that much, even with Mom. She would tell me about how dad was in the army during WWII. I was a toddler then. He was lucky, never having been deployed into a combat zone. After the war, dad had a lengthy career in civil service. The base he worked at was closed due to defense cutbacks, and dad was able to take an early retirement.

Toward the end of his life, dad finally began to talk about his life prior to enlisting in the service. One very gray Saturday morning, I was visiting with dad in the nursing home where he resided. Mom had not accompanied me that day. She was going to visit with an old friend, and they were going to get their hair done later that afternoon. I took a seat next to the rocking chair he was sitting in and listened to dad tell me about a very dark, sinister part of his early past.

Growing up, Dad had three brothers and three sisters. That part I knew about. I did not know that both of his parents died soon after his twelfth birthday of scarlet fever. For the next four years, he was raised by his oldest brother, Charlie, and his older sister, Elizabeth, everybody called her Elsie.

Son, I was very angry after the death of my folks. Daddy was a part-time preacher and full-time schoolteacher. Momma worked in the school office. We had a pretty good life living on our small hobby farm. We had chickens, goats, and pigs once and a while. I liked working with the livestock. One year, I raised a runt pig that Momma sow culled out and stopped feeding. I cried and cried when he was too big to keep. Daddy took me aside and told me that Scotty, that's what I named him, was a gift from God. His sacrifice would provide nourishment for our bodies. Scotty's spirit would never really disappear. It would be passed on to us. Those were very kind words, but I still refused to eat any part of him.

They both died from the fever just two days apart. The strange thing was the rest of us were never sick for a day. The county wanted all the minor children to go into foster care, but my oldest brother, Charlie, told the judge he would be our legal guardian and raise us. I'm afraid I wasn't much help. Your uncle Eric and I were always getting into trouble at school. When I turned sixteen, I finally took off for good. I jumped into a moving freight car and was off to see the great big world. I did not return home for three years. I discovered very quickly that the world was a very evil place, full of bad, ruthless people who saw no value in friendship. Many of them would just rob you and leave you for dead. On my second night hoboing, I got robbed, beat up, and tossed off the train I was riding on.

I rolled down the embankment and banged into a big pine tree. I was cold and hungry. I walked for quite a while before coming up to a farmhouse. It was almost dusk, and everyone was inside. So, I helped myself to a couple of blankets hanging on a clothesline. I snatched them off the line and ran. Then I ran some more before I finally looked back to see if anyone was following me. I scampered down deep in a patch of woods. I was starving, so I started gathering up pinecones looking for pine nuts that the squirrels missed. I found a few, but I was still hungry. I looked around. The only light was from a quarter moon surrounded by an endless overlay of stars. Daddy used to talk about the celestial bodies in the heavens. I missed Daddy and Momma so much, especially when I was hoboing.

What a dangerous and lonely life I had chosen to embark upon. As I lay under the blankets I stole, I wiped across my stomach with my hand. I lifted up my shirt, and there was a huge black and purple bruise just below my ribcage where I bounced off that big pine tree. My knee was sore where the asshole that swiped all my food kicked me. Then he proceeded to toss me off the train. All I asked him was if he wanted to trade some of his drink for a portion of my food. He jumped up and kicked me in the knee. When I dropped my bag, he grabbed it, threw it behind him, and ten seconds later, I flew out the rail car door, so much for romantic adventures riding on the rails. I had to grow up real fast. That incident was my wakeup call. From then on, I had to be very cautious when approaching strangers. I quickly became a very light sleeper.

I witnessed a man being raped and murdered by another man. I say, man, but honestly, the one being raped was a boy probably younger than me. I watched in disgust, scared to make a sound. I know I should have intervened, but I was terrified of being his next victim. I slowly and quietly escaped from that area. I never saw the older man again. I would not have been a witness to anything if it hadn't been for the small campfire burning. I wish I had not been so inquisitive. It took me a long time to rustle that image out of my head. For weeks, I was paranoid that the old man would catch up to me. The only weapon I had was a rusty old pocketknife I had found. Eventually, I got both blades working and made myself a dagger out of a deer antler I happened upon.

It wasn't all bad; after a few months on my own, I learned how not to be seen when I didn't want to. Also, I got really good at hunting small game. I learned how to catch squirrels and rabbits. One time, I was cooking a rabbit, and two older men showed up. I grabbed my bag and blankets and hauled ass. I could always catch something else for dinner.

After a year on my own, I thought seriously about going back home, but I was ashamed of what I had evolved into. I did manage to acquire some accouterments, namely a skillet and hunting knife. I was walking along a creek one very hot afternoon and stumbled upon a young woman swimming in the water. To my delight, she was naked. I had never seen a completely naked girl before. She turned and headed for shore, and I dropped and hid behind some brush.

She called out, "Did you get an eye full?"

I rose up and said, "I saw you naked."

"It's okay honey, lots of men have seen me naked. Are you from around here?"

"No, I am just passing through."

"Well, Just Passing Through, what's your name."

"Darby, my name is Darby."

"How old are you, Darby?"

"Eighteen, I think. I haven't seen a calendar for some time. I don't know what today's date is."

She continued to get dressed and noticed I had a big hard-on. I was so startled by her physique I didn't even know I had one.

"Darby, is that boner of yours on my account." My face was red as a beet, and I quickly turned away.

"Darby, are you a virgin?" I didn't know what to do or what to say. She grabbed my hand, and we walked down the path to a small clearing. We stretched our blankets out on the ground, and she started to undress me.

"Don't be nervous, honey. Everybody has a first time. By the way, my name is Janice."

She crawled on top of me. I was so excited, I didn't know what to think. She rode me for a minute and hopped off. I finished quickly. Then she wiped me off and got on top of me again. After a few minutes, she was done. Then, a minute later, I was done again. That afternoon, she taught me everything I ever wanted to know about sex and making love to a woman.

Even the subtle stuff about how to make it immensely pleasurable for both partners. I finally got up the courage to speak. I asked her if she lived around here.

"No, I travel the rails like you do."

"Janice, how old are you?"

"I am twenty-four."

"Why did you just have sex with me?"

"Darby, you are a very sweet, handsome young man, and someday you are going to get married. I did what I did because I want you to be a generous, gracious husband in your marriage bed. So many men are not, including my former husband. He tried to rape me, and I killed him. That's why I'm here. Darby, you are welcome to tag along with me for a while. Just don't get any foolish notions about owning me. I am nobody's girl, but we can partner up for a while if you like."

"I would like that very much."

I found myself emotionally entangled with Janice. She was older and definitely had that farm-girl appeal. I never had a steady girlfriend back home. I would peek through my sister Elsie's room when she was entertaining her boyfriend. I could not see much through the sheet and blanket. That was my first lesson in sex education. Janice presented me with lessons two through twenty. Her curriculum was much more stimulating.

We hopped rail cars heading west, passing by many Hoovervilles along the way. So many people despair in their circumstances. No money and very little food to speak of to keep them going. I felt bad for the families with small children. Janice and I were lucky in the fact that we were good at foraging. We always seemed to find food somewhere. The winter months were a bit more challenging. Small game was harder to come by.

We found ourselves in the Ozarks during the winter of 1935, living in a makeshift lean-to/shack made of dead logs we were able to gather. It wasn't much, but with the two of us bundled together, it was warm enough. Many nights, the sky was black as molasses with no moon to cast shadows. Having Janice with me made the dangerous life of hoboing seem bearable. We were constantly at the mercy of large apex predators; bears, big cats, wild hogs, and razorbacks were the worst. One night, a wild hog chased us up a tree and would not leave. We had to wait until the beast finally fell asleep at the base of the trunk. I slid down to within six feet of the beast; I drew my knife from its sheath, bit down on the back of the blade, secured it in my mouth, and swooped down on the animal. I grabbed my knife again and thrust it into the side of the hog's neck. It rolled over on me and tried to stand. Then all four legs went spread eagle, and it ceased to move. I severed the head off as fast as I could. Janice and I butchered all the meat we could carry and left hastily before another big predator caught the scent. That hog kept us in meat almost the rest of the winter. Those ribs were a very welcome change from all the hares and chipmunks we were living on. Our bellies were full for the first time in months.

It made the snow baths we took almost bearable. You sort of get used to it after a while. I think the thing that I missed the most was fresh ground coffee. We had been living on tree-bark coffee for months. Janice and I were ready for spring. The ground was still frozen deep. It would be weeks before the winter thaw. Janice seemed to be restless, living so isolated. I kept telling her we were safe up here. If we try to go down to the valley too soon, we will struggle foraging down there. No one knows we are up here, and that gives us a big advantage.

"Come on, Darby, let's go down to the valley. I need to see people again. I want real food for a change. We can sell the rabbit pelts and head back east."

"No, it's too risky. You remember the last time you went into town and tried to have a good time. You damn near killed that old man after he grabbed your ass. You were lucky that jagged, broken bottle didn't nick his jugular vein when you swiped it across his neck. If that guy had died, we would both be in jail."

"I know, but I'm really bored."

"Why don't you work on your rabbit fur coat? It's almost done."

"Okay."

I thought that was the end of it, but she took off on me sometime early the next morning. I looked up and saw that all the pelts and smoked meats were gone. I could not believe she just lit out with all the extra rations. All she left me were the contents of my possibles bag. I was pissed. That would only keep me going for a few days. Well, lesson learned, don't trust anyone out there.

She will always be my first love, and I am eternally grateful for that. I just wish her running out on me hadn't hurt so bad. Janice gave me lots of firsts, heartache among them. She was a handful during the day but conjugal at night. Constantly horny. We could never pass a swimming hole without going skinny dipping. That was definitely her thing. That said, I was still really ticked at her for stealing all the supplies. I had to hunt every day to keep from going hungry. I wasn't planning to go anywhere until the spring thaw. I really had to scavenge for that last month of winter. I just didn't see that one coming.

I managed to find enough game to keep me going by rationing everything I had. When I did finally make it to the valley, I saw no sign of Janice. I decided right then I was going to swallow my pride and go back home where I belonged. Three years of living homeless and broke was enough to make me realize that family was more important to me than freedom. Freedom comes at a price, and right now, it's more than I can afford.

Charlie was so glad to see me. I didn't quite know what to expect, running off the way I did. I figured he and my other siblings would be sore at me for abandoning them. I walked through the front door, and we all had a big group hug. Then they held their noses and pointed to the bathroom upstairs. I went up straightaway and scoured off all the stench. As I laid back in the claw foot tub, soaking in the nice warm bubble bath, I thought to myself, suburbia isn't so bad. I don't smell like a hibernating bear anymore. Then I got a whiff of supper cooking in the kitchen. Fried chicken, mashed potatoes, gravy, greens, black-eyed peas, buttered biscuits, etc. I was really home. I didn't elaborate on how bad it was living on my own. I never mentioned the bar fights, petty thefts, and the murder I saw first-hand. I figured, why ruin their vicarious adventure? I did tell my brothers about Janice, though. So now you know everything, son. The world can be a cruel, a hellish place or a garden paradise. It all depends greatly upon who and how you express yourself at any given point. If you live your life surrounded by good people, chances are you will be blessed.

Daddy passed away two months later. I never repeated to anyone what Daddy told me that day, but I suspected that Mom knew about the conversation. I remember a comment Mom made at Daddy's memorial service.

She said, "Your Daddy and I shared a wonderful life together. You know as well as I do that his entire life was not that way." She reached over and put my hand in hers. "He was such a sweet, dutiful husband. I wanted for nothing." I handed her a tissue, and she wiped away her tears. Mom surpassed Dad by almost ten years. She kept her cosmetics business going for a couple of years after Daddy died. I begged her to sell the business and retire. Finally, she did. That was another good day for me.

Chapter 11: A Marriage on the Brink

Joey walked down the ramp, exiting the plane. He was still wearing a boot cast, but, looked good all the same. It was a short drive from Denver to Colorado Springs. The Rockies were always beautiful in spring. The crisp air and distant snowcaps were something I always enjoyed every time I went there. Rachel was waiting for Joey and I at her condo. We were invited to lunch. Apparently, Joey had spoken with her just prior to our arrival because I thought she was going to suck his face off when he walked in the door. I just looked away at the mountains in the distance for a few moments.

"Okay, we're done, Dad. I would like you to meet Rachel, my fiancée."

I took one look at her and thought to myself all of my grandchildren are going to be supermodels. She was stunning. Then she kissed me on the cheek and told me to come on in. I expected to see a bunch of cats and dogs running around. Not one pet. I found that interesting and very refreshing. I was really taken back by how beautiful this woman was. As we sat down to dinner I started asking about a million questions.

"It is okay, Dad. Is it alright if I call you Dad?"

"Yes, please do."

"I grew up in Denver, my parents Dean and Hallie are still alive and have been married to one another for thirty-two years. They live in Denver. I Went to Vet school at the Colorado Hills College. After graduation, I got an offer from the Clinic I work at now and I've been there ever since. Joey and I met at a cowboy dance club downtown. Your son is a pretty good dancer."

"He didn't inherit that skill from me because when it comes to dancing, I have two left feet with my shoelaces tied together. Colorado is such a beautiful, pristine place to live; I can see why your folks settled here. Have you and joey set a date yet?"

"No, tentatively, we are thinking June or July. It's beautiful here in the summer. We both want a simple ceremony. Just the immediate family. There are several parks around here. We can use Pikes Peak as a backdrop. That's how I want to begin my journey with your son. Dad, you raised a wonderful, kind, loving man. There is no other person on this earth I would want to spend the rest of my life with."

Joey sniffled, "Honey, you are going to make me cry. I just hope I can live up to that rousing endorsement."

"You better because I intend to reciprocate in the same way."

"Son, I don't mind telling you she is a keeper. I could not be happier for both of you. I don't mean to be pessimistic, but I don't honestly know if Sue will be well enough to attend the wedding. Are you aware of my wife's mental illness?"

"Well, I know she suffers from schizophrenia, which is complicated by manic depression. She seems to be doing slightly better since hearing that Joey is no longer missing. Frankly, I am glad I was unaware of the entire incident. We didn't exactly separate on good terms. I would have probably blamed myself in some way. Thank God he is a survivor. Although with two toes missing, Joey isn't going to run a five-minute mile anymore. Maybe I can catch up to him now. The V A still wants to operate on that foot again, don't they?"

"Yes, they do. They think that it will give a lot more mobility. The surgeon was very optimistic when I spoke to him last month. They want to do the preop in Denver six weeks from now."

I asked Joey, "Have you given any thought to what you want to do after the army?"

"Yes, I want to go to chef school here in Colorado. I love to cook. Either that or be a mercenary in South America. A short, uncomfortable silence fell over the room. Just kidding! Seriously, I did receive a call from an international private security firm, to work for them as a training advisor. The guy said I would be behind a desk. Mostly I would be writing equipment and training manuals. There would be lots of room for advancement, they're officed here in Colorado Springs, and the starting pay is very attractive. They try to hire as many special forces officers and NCOs as they can. The recruiter told me I would be looking at a salary close to 75K to start."

"Honey, there's no chance you would ever be assigned to fieldwork, is there?"

"That's the real question. I asked him the same thing."

"What did he say?"

"He said no."

"Do you believe him; do you trust him?"

"I have a friend who recently retired from the Army as a full Colonel, living in Seattle. One of his last official acts was to recommend me for OCS. He gave my name to the recruiter."

"Can you trust this colonel?"

"Yes, certainly more than the recruiter."

"I will give him a call later. I am sorry, Dad, you were giving us an update on Mom's condition."

"Ok, Mom is eating on her own and starting to gesture compliance or non-compliance with a nod. This started soon after the doctors told her Joey was alive and doing good. It may be some time before Sue is ready to join me again. I have to be honest; I doubt she will be able to attend your wedding. Personally, I can't wait to watch you two tie the knot. So far, Sue hasn't spoken a word since the attempted suicide. I am ever hopeful that Joey might bring her back to us. When the staff mentions his name, she does perk up a bit, but she has said nothing yet."

"When are you guys heading to Texas?"

"Soon. I assume you two want a little time to get reacquainted. I will make myself very comfortable in a nearby hotel."

"No way, I just spent almost a grand furnishing the guestroom. You are staying right here, sir."

"Let me grab my bag out of the car."

"Stop. Joey, make yourself useful and get the bags out of the car. Dad, follow me downstairs. I will show you to your room." We walked into the guestroom. It was adorned with all manner of fly-fishing decor, right down to the fly rod rack in the corner.

"I was a bit of a tomboy growing up. My dad, Dean, taught me how to fly-fish almost before I could walk. I love flying almost as much as that big lug bringing the bags in the house."

"I have a boat that I keep in Galveston. You teach me to fly-fish, and I will take you deep sea fishing."

"I will introduce you to my dad, and he will have you going in no time. He taught me everything I know."

"It's a deal. Is that a king salmon you are hoisting in that picture?

"Yes, that was one of our Oregon trips. Personally, I like fishing in the Grand Tetons in Idaho. It's breathtaking up there."

"Joey didn't mention you liked fly-fishing."

"That's because Joey stinks at it. He keeps putting the fly in his ear. He may as well wear them as earrings. On the next trip, we will bring him along to cook for us. We have a cabin on thirty acres in Idaho. My folks have civil service jobs at the Denver Mint. Dad is retiring next year. Mom is scheduled to retire the following year. Then, they will be spending lots of time in Idaho. We refer to it as a cabin, but it's more of a lodge. It has six bedrooms and three bathrooms. They built it on stilts to account for all the snow and apex game in the area, including wolves. It's only eighty miles from Yellowstone Park. God, I love it up there. I owe a ton of great weekends to that place. I hope you like fish and fowl. We only eat what we hunt and catch."

"Has Joey seen this place yet?"

"No, not yet, but he will see it soon enough. Once he gets up there, he may never want to leave. I know he's a fantastic hunter."

"Yes, and he is easily the best marksman I have ever seen. He only needs one bullet to go hunting."

"Up there, that's a very good thing."

"Here's your bag, sir. Do you want it on the bed?"

"Yes, thank you. Rachel tells me you finally found something you suck at."

"Ok! Ok, I freely admit that I really stink at fly-fishing. Fine. Go ahead and poke fun at my only fault!" I just fell back on the bed laughing. I think he and Rachel are going to be very happy together. I wish them all the luck in the world.

Today is another extremely good day. Lately, it is getting as though I only get a handful every passing year. I sit in the chair adjacent to the window in the guestroom, staring up at Pikes peak in the distance, supposing what will happen when Sue sets her eyes on Joey. I pray she starts talking again. We will both know in about a week.

Joey hasn't talked too much about reconnecting with Sue. I hope he doesn't get overwhelmed at the moment. If he can handle the streets of Baghdad, he can deal with Mom. I should try and feel him out and see where his thoughts are. To be honest, I'm not sure where my thoughts will be when I see her again. The conversations I had with her attending physician have not been very optimistic to this point, less the fact that she is eating on her own again. It would appear to a layman like me that she has lost her will to connect. In a way, I was lucky. I had to focus so much on Sue and her welfare I was separated from the fact that Joey was laying somewhere under several feet of snow.

I walked into the kitchen, sat down, grabbed a chocolate chip cookie from a bowl on the dining room table, and took a bite. Delicious.

"Rachael, did you make these?"

"I wish. They are incredible. I buy them at a bakery around the corner." Joey sat down and polished off two of them. "Joey, do you mind telling me how you got out of that avalanche?"

"Sure, Dad. It was Saturday, I had just finished cleaning all cold weather gear and getting ready to do some laundry in the barracks when I heard this loud snap. At first, I thought it was artillery, but as far as I knew, we didn't have any. Then I heard rumbling. Everyone looked out the window for a moment. Then I heard someone scream, 'AVALANCHE!!' We all crawled under our bunks. Then, the room imploded. The roof caved in, and I could barely move. I started to crawl for the door, then let out a loud scream. I looked down at my leg, and it was broken. I could see the bone just barely exposed. There was snow everywhere. I oriented myself the best I could and started crawling toward where I thought the door was. I knew my leg was in a world of hurt. The bleeding stopped, probably from the cold. I started to hear voices behind me, and then I saw Wills and Barton. They tunneled through the snow like I did. They both had severe cuts and bruises everywhere. Wills had a broken hand. He strapped it to his waist using his belt. Barton lost an eye. It was completely missing from the socket. We were in bad shape. If they didn't find us soon we were done for. Wills passed out after about an hour. He never woke up. Barton and I kept crawling to where we expected the door to be. I pushed my hand as far as I could forward, and I felt the snow push away from me. As I scooted and scraped the snow away there was a small area that was clear. I dragged Barton through the snow tunnel I made into this spot. The roof truss had severed and crashed to the ground. In doing so, it stopped the snow from filling up a small area about twelve by twelve. I could feel a slight breeze coming from somewhere.

That was good news because it meant we had airflow. That gave us precious time. It was cold, but we were both fully clothed, and the surrounding snow wasn't melting yet. We had all the water we needed to survive for days in the form of snow. But it all depended on how long it would take to be rescued. Our unit wasn't due for a radio check for another forty-eight hours. Headquarters would not check on us until then. Barton and I knew we were going to get really cold and hungry before this was over. We checked each other out for critical injuries. Except for my broken leg, his broken collarbone, and missing eye, we weren't that bad off. Now, we just had to wait. Neither of us was in any shape to try and venture very far. I knew there would be a rescue party coming in three days. Barton and I got to know each other really well, having nothing but shared body heat to keep us from freezing to death. On the third day I noticed I had no pain in some of my toes. That means frostbite.

On day five, we heard machinery. It was useless to bang on anything; they couldn't hear us over the bulldozers anyhow. Night six was the worst. Barton was getting really sick from exposure. I couldn't feel any of my toes at this point. The next thing I remember is waking up in the base hospital a week later. My right leg was set in a cast, and two toes were missing. I thought, well, my army career is officially over. I asked the doctor how Barton was. He told me Barton was still in ICU but stable. Barton was in ICU another week before he woke from his induced coma. Now I'm here. I have no desire to go to Alaska again. I don't even want to fly over that place. Barton and I were the only survivors. We were damn lucky. The other fourteen men on that training mission all died. All the bodies were recovered.

I was so scared and cold that I thought I was going to die a slow, cold death. It was worse than having a gun pointed at my head, which also happened a few times. Truly, that was scary, but hearing the machines running, trying desperately to find us, was overwhelming. My injuries made me helpless in harsh surroundings. Cold, just really cold and scared. Really fuckin scared. (barely sobbing) I did what I had to do and survived."

Joey sat there and composed himself. Neither Rachel nor I said a word. We just watched the man morph out of that hellish cocoon of terror and come back to us straight away. I raised one tough SOB.

"That is pretty much what I told my shrink. He told me the more I talk about it, the better off I will be later. Talking helps. Now, we just have to get Mom to let go and start speaking to us. Now, when do you want to head out to see Mom?"

"Next week, the last report I got from her doctor was a little more encouraging."

"That's good news."

"Yes, it is."

Chapter 12: Lessons in Sacrifice

I watched Rachel and Joey neck in the doorway of her condo for what seemed like ten minutes. That was some powerful kissing. I felt like telling him we were going to be back in about two weeks. That's probably how long it will take to wipe the smile off his face. I am glad to see him so happy.

I hope he can remain cheerful after he sees his mother in the insolent state she is in right now. It is not pleasant to see her like that. We headed down I-25 to intersect I-10 and cut through New Mexico. I forgot just how pretty the southwest is. It's hot, really hot, and dry, really dry. It is beautiful and arid. Thank God for air conditioning. Luckily, by the time we got to I-10, the sun was almost down.

I hate rental cars. It never fails to astonish me why it takes almost the entire trip to learn how to drive the damn thing. I would have loved it if Joey drove back to Houston, but he could not be due to his injuries. His physical therapist said it may be a few months before he should get behind the wheel again. That means I get to do all the driving.

"Man, I hate driving on long trips."

"Yes, Dad, I know, so why didn't we fly back?"

"I wanted time to tell you some things about your mom and me that are not common knowledge. I noticed very soon after the honeymoon that Mom struggled with anxiety and depression. I thought it was just her adjusting to married life. I was concerned about starting a family with your mom. She ended up getting pregnant anyway, but it wasn't you she was carrying. Prior to mom's pregnancy with you, there was another, a stillbirth. Kelly Ann would have been your older sister. She died during the third trimester. The autopsy revealed it was an abnormal placenta. I thought my heart was being ripped out through my earhole. I sincerely hope that you never have to experience that kind of heartache. Losing a child, even a stillborn, is a terrible ordeal to live through. You know firsthand that our marriage had issues. I don't believe I ever told you that my parents didn't want me to marry Susan. They saw what I didn't. I knew that she was no scholar, but she was so beautiful I just overlooked everything else. I was a bit naive in that department. Actually, it was her father's drinking that really worried them, but they had no knowledge of the schizophrenia attached to it. Your grandma was always a really good judge of character. I miss her wisdom, charisma, and wit. She could run off some really funny stuff sometimes. She and Dad made quite a career for themselves selling cosmetics door to door. They received several big bonuses over the years.

Soon after Dad passed away, Mom walked me out to the dry goods barn and opened the big safe in the back. The big iron door creaked when I swung it open to reveal twenty white bank envelopes. Each one contained one thousand dollars in cash. Dad told me several times that they had some egg money stashed away. I didn't have any idea it was literally adjacent to the chicken coop. It is very fortunate that no one knew about that. I was flabbergasted when I saw all that cash just sitting there. They were a different generation. Some of those bills were over forty years old. Mom did not put much faith in banks and trusted the government even less. They both grew up in the thirties. It was an interesting drive to the bank. I got Mom to purchase a short-term CD. She groveled a bit about having to pay taxes. Mom calmed down when I told her she only had to pay taxes on the interest the bank paid her.

There was always a regimented coolness between Mom and Sue. She always thought my mom was trying to manipulate her in some way. Honestly, most of the time, your mother was right, and she resented the hell out of that, especially when it came to raising you. Sue hated it when you would go and stay with my folks. She hatched all kinds of ridiculous scenarios in her head that Mom was trying to kidnap you and make you stay there permanently. It was all complete crap. I don't know what your mom's family did to her to make her that way. I suspect they were not very supportive when she was really young. She told me Tess would sometimes punish her severely for minor incidents when her dad would come in late from drinking. Bill would stagger into the house, and your mom would get ostracized for it. That's never a good thing. Mom mentioned that she was molested by an uncle when she was very young. That kind of thing went on quite a bit back then. I have never been able to get her to talk about that. I can't get her to talk about anything. I would love to know what she talked about with her therapist, but Dr. Beck won't break confidentiality. I understand it's better for her that way. Still, it's frustrating not knowing what actually took place during her upbringing."

"Dad, I talked to the shrink about mom when I was stationed in Colorado. I had some questions about Mom's illness. It helped me understand why she acts this way."

"That was smart. It's always good to bring in an expert every once and a while instead of relying on your best educated guess. I have talked to many experts over the years, and some of them have been very helpful, and some have not. The day Mom took all those pills was not a good day. I got an earful of advice. Some of which I could certainly have done without. I had doctors recommending all sorts of treatments for your mom. One suggested a convent in Washington state. Maybe he was figuring that the lack of sex drive might lead her to a life of service. I want her to get better, but I don't want to be married to a nun. I decided on a clinic right outside of Austin. It is only ninety minutes from the house. It seemed like a reasonable compromise. Our insurance paid for most of it as well. Not that I was overly concerned with the price.

"Son, I want to make one thing crystal clear to you. I do not hold you responsible for your mom attempting to take her life. If it hadn't been that incident, it would have been something else. She had been on edge for quite a while up to that point. You have to live your own life. I should also mention that your being involved with another female may not be very comforting for Mom. I mentioned one time that you might be seeing someone in Colorado, and she balked at me. I didn't think too much of it at the time, but now it may be upsetting to her. I don't know. I may be putting too much into it. Either way, you and Rachel have to live your own lives. Don't let anyone dictate to you. Last of all, me or your mom. I got enough of that shit from my mom and dad. I will freely give you advice if you ask for it. Up to that point, you are old enough to stand by your own decisions. I have a question for you, son. What is it about your intended that you find so appealing? Because if it's just the eye candy, that's the wrong answer."

"I thought you weren't going to make any judgments."

"No, you are right, she could be a professional model, but she is not that superficial. At least, I have never seen that side of her. As far as I can tell, she doesn't wear much makeup at all. I agree Rachel is a very attractive woman. Men look and flirt with her all the time, even when I am around. That is something I will have to get used to. Crazy as it sounds, we did not hook up the first night we met. We weren't even on a date. She and I were with different people that night. Tracy, my date that night, I hooked up with, and her roommate. That's another story. I got Rachel's number from Tracy. I played it very cool right from the beginning. I think I might have been a bit intimidated by her looks. We didn't do anything more than kiss until the third date. It was actually kind of nice not being under all that pressure. We definitely have common interests, outdoors, animals, and each other. I feel like she loves me for who I am. When she tells me she loves me, I can see the truth in her eyes. Those beautiful hazel eyes of hers. I am completely taken by her. I want to make her happy."

"Well, you have the financial and commitment angle covered. What about infidelity? She is a ten all day long. You are a nine wannabe."

"Oh, stop busting my chops. We are definitely monogamous. Like I said, I will have to get used to all the glances from other men. As for me, I don't want to be with any other woman." I said that also, and half a dozen affairs later, I just hope he doesn't see the regret in my eyes. If any couple has a chance to stay together, they are off to a really good start.

"Okay, I believe you, but be careful. Sometimes, wanting is not enough. By the way, who is paying for the wedding?"

"I am paying for most of it. Her folks are buying the dress."

"My contribution shouldn't be more than a few thousand."

"We don't want some ridiculous $50,000 theme wedding in Vegas or NYC. That is just not our style. We exchanged portfolios, and Rachel has almost as much squirreled away as I do. She has done very well for herself to this point. My only real concern is Mom. I don't see her making the wedding. I haven't told her folks about Mom yet."

"One or both of us need to tell them as soon as possible. I will go with you. I just hope they understand that you are not like that in any way."

"I met them once; they don't know about the engagement. We haven't had time to go tell them. We seemed to hit it off fairly well. Both her parents had prior service, so the military thing wasn't that big of a deal since, at the time, they thought I was considering OCS. Also, they called me while I was recuperating in the hospital, and both were happy to hear I was going to be making a full recovery. I think they suspect Rachel and I are getting very serious about one another. I believe if the three of us tell her parents about Mom together, they should understand. I want to be as transparent as possible concerning Mom. We need to make this meeting happen soon. I should call Rachel now and get it in the works. Damn, no service on my cell phone. I will have to call from the motel. Speaking of that, how much further to El Paso?"

"About three hours. We will be there just about supper time. Do me a favor. Don't flirt with the waitress this time. You are officially off the market, buddy. Personally, I don't think you will ever find anything better than Rachel, and if I hear you ran around on her, I will remove your manhood and put it in a jar. Kapish."

"Point taken. Okay, I am off the menu. I don't even want a bachelor party. I would love to see the statistics on divorced men who had a wild bachelor party. I bet it's a high percentage. I could never cheat on Rachel. I would never be able to face her. I feel safe and secure when I am with her. This morning, I was sitting in bed watching her get ready for work. She was sitting in a chair in front of the vanity mirror, putting on her earrings. I almost dropped a tear, thinking how lucky I was to be with her. She saw me staring at her and asked me what I was gawking at. I told her, I see something beautiful reflecting back at me. Then she walked over to me, leaned over for a kiss, and said I love the passionate man inside you. Dad, are you crying?"

"I have been unfaithful to your mother. I am sorry, so sorry. Seeing and hearing you talk about Rachel makes me highly regret all the affairs I had. I thought I was justified in straying from our marriage bed due to her lack of sexual desire. I was wrong. Selfish and wrong."

"Dad, you are trapped in a loveless marriage. I don't think anyone would hate you for what you did. Everyone needs to be reminded that they are loved once and a while."

"Kat said the same thing."

"Who is Kat?"

"The most memorable one-night stand I ever had. I know the guilt is parallel with my responsibility to Mom. They stab at my heart like two endless vectors. Circumflecting the earth returning for another blow."

"You are the poster boy for a faithful marriage. Try not to dwell on it. Have you ever told anyone what you told me?"

"Just my therapist, I think."

"I won't tell a soul."

We arrived at the motel and checked in. This was definitely a no-tell motel. The bathroom was clean, and I was asleep as soon as my head hit the pillow. I got up the next morning, washed up, dressed, and walked to the diner next door. As soon as I walked in, I was overwhelmed by the pleasing aroma. I was like, oh yes, they serve breakfast here. I spotted Joey sitting in a booth. I grabbed the seat across from him.

Joey smirked and said, "Good morning, sleepyhead."

"They got any coffee in this place?"

"Oh yeah, it's really good."

"Let's shoot for San Antonio today. Houston is over twelve hours away. I will never make it. I think I slept forever. Why didn't you wake me up?"

"I did. You told me to go amuse myself in a sexual manner."

"Oops, sorry about that. We covered over five hundred miles yesterday. I'm getting old, son. I haven't driven like that in quite some time. Today is a little shorter, thank goodness. Did I really tell you to screw yourself?" He nodded. I looked down at my watch. It was still on central time. I don't have to switch it back. The waitress came by with a mug and a carafe of coffee. "Bless you, madame. Do you have fresh cream?"

"I'll get you some right away. The cow is right out back. Unless you prefer goat's milk?"

"Yes, we are definitely back in Texas." After breakfast we jumped back on the road headed for San Antone.

"Joey, do you want to go see your mom tomorrow on the way home or the next day?"

"Let's go on the way home. We have been on the road enough for me to last quite a spell. Tell me again why you chose to drive."

"I wanted time to talk things out, and we did. I'm sure it was more than either of us expected. That's ok, it was still a very good thing. I hope I didn't dump too much bullshit on you all at once. I felt it was necessary to bring you up to speed on everything. We will probably run into Tess at the clinic. She is there almost every day. That was another reason I picked a clinic in Austin. I figured if Tess was a frequent visitor, it might help Sue to recover. It seems to be working. I'm going to call them from the motel this afternoon. I don't think we should tell her about Rachel yet."

"Pop, we've got to. I'm getting married in less than a year. If not now, when."

"You're right. There is no good time to tell her. May as well get it out on the table."

"Any idea how she will react seeing me?"

"I don't know, and she didn't have much of a reaction to you being alive. Maybe it is just taking time to sink in."

"I hope so. If not, we are in for a rough road ahead."

"That's for sure."

Gassed up and fed, we headed for East Texas. I don't know how the cowboys did it on horseback. I know I would be sitting tall on horseback with chronic saddle sores everywhere. I have never even been on a motorcycle before. That would probably be enough to tear me up. I am terrified of how Sue will react seeing Joey alive. I just hope she doesn't regress back to a catatonic state. She could. Her sense of reality is very fragile right now.

Chapter 13: The Cost of Silence

Joey and I are sitting in the parking lot, procrastinating. We both have butterflies the size of bowling balls rolling around in our stomachs. I am really scared at this point of what will go down once we see Susan. Joey grabbed my arm and said, "Come on, Pop, let's get it over with. We won't accomplish anything by sitting on our asses."

We exited the car and started walking toward the entrance. Just before I opened the outer door, a staff member opened the inner door and hurriedly guided us to Sue's room. Sue jumped up onto Joey's shoulders. All she kept repeating was Joey, Joey, Joey, Joey. After several minutes she finally sat back down in her chair and just gleamed at him. Then she just kept saying, "Joey," repeatedly. The nurse came in and administered a sedative. The orderly transferred her back to her bed, and she finally passed out asleep. It wasn't the response that we were hoping for. She is a long way from cured.

Her primary case worker came into the room and asked us if she could chat with us privately. We scurried down to her office and sat down.

"I am Dr. Ames; it is a great pleasure to finally meet you, Joey. I heard about your ordeal in Alaska. How is your recovery going?"

"I am good, thank you for asking."

"Gentlemen, let me be candid. That was not the reaction we were expecting or hoped for. Hopefully, this is just a temporary lapse. Susan had been making slight progress off and on ever since we found out that you survived your ordeal. At this point it probably isn't a good idea that she sees you again, for a while. I'm so sorry."

I interjected, "It seems that would be best."

"Doctor, would it be permissible for me to sit quietly in her room?"

"Mr. Stockton, please stay as long as you like."

"Call me Joey, thank you." Joey walked out of the room and headed down the hall. I remained seated.

"Doctor Ames, how long?"

"We are very informal around here. Please call me Melissa."

"Melissa, how long?"

"I don't know, a year maybe more. Her mental condition doesn't start and stop with schizophrenia. She has an extremely hard time dealing with the loss of a loved one. Her chart indicates major episodes with the passing of her brother and father. It doesn't indicate suicide attempts back then, but I suspect she was contemplating it. You were there when she tried to overdose, weren't you? Did she say anything just prior to the attempt?"

"All I can recall was getting her a glass of wine in the kitchen. When I returned to the patio, she was already upstairs, sitting on the edge of the bed with half a bottle of pills in her hand. I grabbed her and hauled ass. She said nothing in the car. That's pretty much how it went down. Sorry, I can't be more help. What exactly are you looking for?"

"Anything that ties this episode to some major trauma in her past."

"There was a conversation the three of us had after Joey enlisted but had not reported yet. Sue yelled out, 'Do you want to get killed like my brother!' That's the only connection I can think of."

"It is a start for me anyway. Take one of my cards, if you think of anything else, call me day or night. It could be significant."

"You got it, doc." I left her office and walked into Sue's room. Joey was sitting in a chair next to the bed with his hands cupped over his face. He pulled his hands away. I could tell he was crying for a bit. This is the first time since the police episode that he saw how damaged Sue had become. What the hell do I do now? Right now, I have no hope for some damn miracle recovery. I'm sure trying to tie the suicide attempt to a previous incident isn't going to amount to shit. Getting pissed off ain't gonna do any good. We ended up hanging around for another forty-five minutes. I drove both of us home. I made this trip so many times I am starting to recognize the house numbers. Dr Ames was new. She must have just started working there. I don't remember ever meeting her before. None of the other staff ever asked for feedback from me. It was refreshing to see a little dedication to one's work.

I did have a thought when I got home. I called the Doc and mentioned I remembered a few things concerning her brother. She suggested we meet somewhere between Austin and Houston so neither of us had to make the long trip. We met at a diner approximately halfway. I started commenting on how Sue and her brother Billy slept together in the same room almost until they were teenagers.

"I was curious as to if they were doing any heavy petting with each other. Sue was very upset when Billy was drafted into Vietnam. He ended up getting killed during the Tet Offensive in 1968. She was very hot and cold on the subject. I never saw her cry much, even at his funeral. People grieve in different ways, but I wondered if claiming she was abused by an uncle was a ruse to cover up incest. When Sue's father passed away a few years later, it hit her hard. With her dad, I think it was more mental cruelty than incest. That's just my uneducated opinion."

"Don't sell yourself short; firsthand knowledge can be extremely useful in formulating a correct diagnosis. That is why I wanted to meet you face to face. Vocabulary and body language can be very revealing."

"I was planning to come to Austin after I escorted Joey back to Colorado. Why all the cloak and dagger stuff?"

"I wanted to interview you out of your element to get a better understanding of your situation. I see you raised an incredible human being despite your handicap (i.e. Susan). You have obviously done well financially to afford our facility. So, I deduced that you are a very well-grounded person."

"I guess I'm a little slow on the uptake. Are you hitting on me?"

"Yes, I find you distinguished, handsome, and interesting. I would like to get to know you better. I completely understand if you are not interested in me, but earlier, when I met you, I was intrigued."

"Melissa, how old are you?"

"Don't tell anyone, but I am thirty-eight."

"Wow, okay, I would have guessed early twenties. You are a very beautiful woman. The fact remains that I am still married to Sue. Plus, I am forty-nine, eleven years your senior, and you look my son's age. I don't know if I want to complicate my life that much."

"Bobby, you are in a loveless marriage. Don't you have needs and desires?"

"Sure, I do, and I have been down that road with other women. Those relationships always leave me a broken man. I am extremely flattered, though. You are stunning."

"Tell me honestly, how long has it been for you?"

"Over ten years. It has been so long I may have forgotten how."

"What have you been doing for ten years?"

"Fishing and Tennis, and work, lots of work."

"Can we at least share a meal together right now?"

"Sure, I can do that without having to sequester my virtue," I told Melissa how I was deeply remorseful over my one-night stand with Kat. I felt like I was taking advantage of this woman's generous nature by listening to my struggles with infidelity to the point of surreal. The more I talked to her, the more I was intrigued by her presence. The contours of her face, her perfume, her presumed cleavage behind that satin blouse that I wanted to unbutton and reveal for my lustful gaze. I told myself that I needed to remain true to Susan for the rest of our so-called marriage. If for nothing else, my own fragile sanity at this point. We left the diner and walked to the sports bar next door. After a couple of cocktails and several hours of conversation, we ended up back at the diner. I needed time to sober up before the hour-and-a-half drive back home. We agreed to talk more. Just talk. Maybe I just needed time to allow the fact I am still attractive to younger women. Melissa was surprisingly respectful to me, turning down her proposal.

A relationship with Melissa could never work. She was too close to Susan. I would think it would be a conflict of interest for her. I think I might have avoided a cougar in reverse. I guess that would be a gold digger. She doesn't seem the type.

I was in the middle of doing laundry, my least favorite thing in life. I heard a knock at the door. I opened the door, and two very distinguished men introduced themselves as Houston Police Detectives. They asked if they could come in and speak to me for a moment. I obliged and closed the door behind them.

"Gentlemen, what can I do for you today."

"Mr. Stockton, have you ever seen this woman before?" One of the men showed me a picture of Melissa with different colored hair. I told them she was a caseworker at the facility where my wife currently resides.

"Sir, you may want to sit down." I sat down.

"What's going on, fellas?" They gave each other a stern gaze and then proceeded to tell me that Dr. Melissa Ames is Abagail Beaker out of Tampa, Florida.

"She is a professional con artist. It appears you were her next victim. Over the last twelve years, she has stolen over eight million dollars from unsuspecting men like you. Have you noticed any suspicious activity in your financials lately?"

"None."

"How long have you been involved with Abagail."

"Days yesterday, we met at a diner halfway between here and Austin to discuss my wife's illness."

"Did she seem interested in you socially?"

"Very much so, and I got a little suspicious. I thought it was very unethical and probably a conflict of interest for her. She did seem very sincere, though. All we did was talk for over six hours. No BS, she really is a con artist."

"Yes, she is even a murder suspect in Maryland."

"Damn, wow, looks like I dodged a bullet. She didn't try to do me any harm, that I can tell. Is she in custody?"

"No, someone tipped her off, and she managed to flee the state undetected. She has people helping her everywhere. Abagail is considered armed and dangerous, so if she should contact you again, call this number immediately. There is a federal warrant for her arrest. There is also a reward for her capture. Consider yourself fortunate; she has ruined hundreds of lives."

I thanked the detectives and closed the door behind them. I immediately went upstairs and relayed all this information to Joey. If I had met Abagail five years ago, I would be in a world of hurt. I sat down, and we watched a basketball game together.

"Dad, can we go and see Mom tomorrow?"

"Sure, I want to talk to the administrator of that facility, and they better have some answers for me, or I am going to raise a huge stink."

We headed out early for Austin and arrived before lunch. There was no change in Sue's condition, but she isn't repeating everything anymore. I guess that is progress. Joey tried to tell Sue he was going to get married, but it was pointless. She acknowledged his presence, but that was all. I met with the facility administrator, Dr. Demore. She was a nice woman; she was so apologetic for what happened and promised to make sure that Sue received the best of care while in residence at the facility. That was pretty much all I wanted. She must have thought I was going to hit them with a lawsuit. Why turn an unfortunate event into a three-ring circus? It's not worth it. However, it would bring a spotlight on Abagail, wherever she is. I'm sure she will get caught sooner or later.

I didn't feel like driving back home that evening, so we stayed in a motel and headed back to Houston the next morning. I took Joey out fishing on the gulf in my boat the following day. It felt good to get back out on the water. The fish weren't really biting. I didn't care; I just wanted to go for a boat ride. We returned to the Marina just before sundown and popped over to the beach. The ocean breeze felt grand. I could taste the salt in the air. If there weren't so many hurricanes, I would just move to Galveston and be done with it. It's okay, I don't mind the drive. The next morning, Joey and I hopped on a plane to Denver.

Chapter 14: A Son's Struggle

Rachel and her parents met us at the airport. Then we headed to her folk's place. They had a nice ranch house with a steep roof, sitting on ten acres. A very nice home. Lots of character. We went inside and sat around the stonework fireplace. Mom and Rachel served light refreshments; then, we began to explain the depths of Susan's mental illness. They were polite but concerned that it was hereditary. After explaining how alcoholism played a part, Dean and Hallie started to understand that any children that may come about from the marriage will probably not be affected in any way. That seemed to be their biggest fear. I told them that the biggest issue Joey and Rachel will have to contend with will be why Susan will not be in attendance for the wedding. I think these two are going to make some gorgeous grandbabies.

"Ok, pop, we'll see." After a nice visit, Rachel, Joey and I headed for Colorado Springs. Rachel's folks were great. They were good people. I can't wait to call them family. We got back to Rachel's condo and settled in for the evening. I sat by the guestroom window again, gazing at Pike's Peak until dusk. I could never get tired of watching that. I walked into the living room and caught the kids necking on the couch. I told them to get a room, and that is exactly what they did. I didn't see them until the next morning. I woke up early. I'm sure it was jet lag. I found Joey sitting at the dining room table, deep in thought. I sat down beside him and grabbed a cookie.

Then I asked Joey, "What's on your mind, son?"

"Pop, you don't think Mom's condition is hereditary."

"Truthfully, it can be, but you have not been exposed to any of the critical stress situations that Mom has. You don't have any latent issues with the loss of family members. You certainly don't have any issues with paranoia or depression that I have seen."

"No, but the thing that scares me is the combat stuff. I had to kill three people during my deployment. Two with a rifle and one with a knife. I am worried that it may come back to haunt me later."

"Have you talked to a counsellor about this?"

"Not since the hospital."

"Any weird dreams or nightmares?"

"No."

"You are going to be okay. Do yourself a favor and make a phone call to the V A. Don't worry so much. As long as you are proactive with your mental health counseling, everything should work itself out."

"I'm scared, Dad; what if I flashback sleeping next to Rachel? What about children? I couldn't handle raising a child with a severe mental illness."

"You are talking about stuff that is years away. Cut yourself some slack. It sounds like you have a big case of pre-wedding heebie jeebies. Let me ask you another question. Have you decided to go to chef school or take the security job?"

"Actually, I was thinking about going to chef school, you know, Culinary Arts. I love to cook. I get off on watching people eat what I make."

"When did you start cooking?"

"In the army I read a bunch of cookbooks and manuals in order to prepare for cold ration bivouacs. The guys in my unit told me I had a knack for it. I was sort of the unofficial unit chef. I cooked for everybody, and the guys would service my gear for me. I want to pursue a career in Culinary. That is where my passion lies."

"Any thought as to what school."

"Denver has an excellent one. Do you think Rachel's folks would let me stay with them while I am in school?"

"I don't see why not."

"I already discussed this with Rachel. She thinks it is a great idea, after busting my balls, saying how, if I can't catch any fish, then I should learn how to cook them. She does have a devious side to her. I never get away with anything. We also discussed putting off the wedding until I finish school. That way, it will be less of a distraction. I hope to be employed as a chef by the time we get hitched. This week, I am going to meet with one of the school advisors to discuss tuition, academic enrollment, etc."

"Do you need a ride up there?"

"That would be great if you could, so Rachel doesn't have to take any time off from work. By the way, my boot cast comes off next week. My leg is almost healed. Then, I can start working out again. I can't wait to get rid of this stupid thing. Before you say anything, yes, I will make an appointment with a VA psychologist."

"Okay, chef, how's about a little dinner."

"We have some ribeye steaks in the freezer. I will go ahead and thaw them out. They should be marinated and ready to broil when Rachel walks through the door. How does sauteed asparagus and homemade mac-n-cheese sound?"

"You really do have a gift for culinary, don't you? That sounds delicious."

"Well, I had help. I used to watch Mom cook in between her mental episodes, and I picked up several things when I used to stay with Grandma Tess during the summer. You and I both know she is still the best scratch cook in Texas, or at least in the top five. I memorized her chili and stew recipes. We both know how amazing her fried chicken is. I am not allowed to divulge that recipe, even under pain of death. She made me take an oath."

"Come on, son, how about just one ingredient? Surely you can slip that to me."

"Okay, one key ingredient is… Paprika. That's all I'm saying. I am sure she probably has a microphone hidden somewhere. Not another word. You know what grandma is like. She will pit devils and saints against one another to get her point across. I need a drink."

"You really are paranoid. It's 1:30 in the afternoon."

"I don't care. Do you want one?"

"Pour me one too. Tess can be very scary at times. It makes me wonder what exactly did go on in that house of hers. When I would spend time with Sue and her family, everything seemed pretty okay, I remember a few elevated conversations. I noticed Tess was always waiting for Bill Sr. to return home. Thinking back, I may have missed some signs of verbal abuse. I can't say conclusively, but there is good circumstantial evidence that she was being bullied in that house. In thirty years of marriage, I can't remember her standing up to anyone except you when you were young. That may be one reason why she babies you so much. Speaking of that, I got a message from the administrator that Mom had some kind of minor breakthrough. She is engaging in conversation again. Sue still can't remember much, and she is really slow to pick up on things, but apparently, she is talking again. It would be a good idea if you accompanied me to Austin."

"Can Rachel accompany us there as well? Do you think Mom can handle meeting her right now?"

"I can find out. I will call Dr. Demore right now."

"Hello, Dr. Demore speaking."

"Dr. Demore, this is Bobby Stockton, I have a question. Given my wife's current state, do you think it would be okay for my son's fiancée to accompany us back to Austin and pay Sue a visit early next week?"

"Well, yes. It may be contentious, but I believe it will be beneficial in the long run. More than likely, Susan will be distant and curt to her and possibly to everyone after they meet. Bring some flowers that may help. Unscented, of course."

"We will do that. See you soon."

Click.

"What did she say, Pop?"

The front door popped open, and Rachel walked in. "I had to leave work early. Somebody brought their pet skunk into the clinic, and it let one go in the lobby. We are going to be closed for three days and won't open until Monday. Did you plan anything for dinner yet?"

"Yes, sweetheart, I am going to broil some ribeye steaks."

"Yum!"

"Honey, Mom had a mild breakthrough. She is talking again. How would you like to accompany Dad and me to Austin and meet her?"

"Is she ready for that?"

I interjected, "Yes, but it could be confrontational. Sue may not be ready to share Joey's affections with another woman. The doc said it would help her in the long run."

"I will go. She has to meet me sooner or later. It just so happens I have a few days off. Maybe we can sneak in a fishing trip on your boat."

"You bet."

"Joey, are you making asparagus and mac-n-cheese to go with the steaks."

"Of course."

"Dad, you're in for a treat; your son cooks better than a restaurant chef. I am going to shower and dress for dinner."

We all sat down for dinner. Joey poured out a nice table Merlot. The steak was absolutely incredible, better than a Kansas City steak house. It had been a long time since I had a meal even close to that calibre. Joey is going to do amazingly well in Chef College. I half stretched out on the couch. I woke up early the next morning to the smell of sizzling bacon and coffee. I peeked over the back of the sofa and there was my dutiful son walking my way with a mug of coffee. I sat up on the couch and discovered under a comfy flannel blanket, I was only wearing my underwear. I slept on the couch all night. I haven't really gotten used to the air up here or the lack of it.

"Pop, that couch sleeps pretty well, doesn't it? Breakfast will be ready in a few minutes. What do you want on your omelet? Or do you want a Denver?"

"Denver is good, thanks. Son, you didn't really learn how to cook like this in the army."

"Sort of, I read several cookbooks cover to cover. It makes a big difference."

"Yes! It does. I would like to fly down to Austin Friday if that works for the both of you." Rachel walked into the room and affirmed as she sat down at the table.

"Hey, gorgeous, tell the truth, you're marrying my son for his cooking skills, right?"

"Yes, but the kitchen isn't the only room in the house where he cooks."

"Ew, TMI, TMI!"

"Sorry, Dad."

"Son, how do you brew such good coffee?"

"No way, Rachel can't even get that secret out of me."

"Forget it." Joey served the omelets and bacon. I devoured it and thought really hard about eating my napkin, too. My mind started to wonder if we could wait a week before going to Texas. No, we had to get down their great cuisine or not. Come Friday morning, we flew out of Denver to Austin.

Chapter 15: The Burden of Love

The Austin airport was twenty minutes away from the mental facility Sue occupied. I was hesitant but optimistic. Dr. Demore met us in the hall.

She said, "Let me go in first, Susan has been rather difficult ever since we told her about Rachel. I will try to lighten the mood before you enter."

The doctor summoned us into the room. I introduced Rachel to Sue, and she said, "Hi."

Rachel said, "Hello, Mrs. Stockton. My name is Rachel. It is an honor to meet you."

"Why would you say that?"

"Any woman who brought Joey into the world deserves my respect and admiration. These flowers are for you."

"It is my understanding that you and Joey want to get married. It seems obvious why my little Joey wants to marry you. You're way too pretty for him. You are just a stunning piece of ass to him. He has had lots of women like you. You should leave now and save yourself lots of pain and heartache. Wouldn't you agree?"

"Well, you have some very strong opinions about your son's love life. You are right. Most people consider me attractive. Joey does, too. I have considered the possibility that Joey is only interested in my body, and he may be trying to corral a trophy wife. I am willing to give him the benefit of the doubt."

"Be careful; my condition will haunt my little Joey for the rest of his life. If you bear my son any children, they will be damaged goods. They will be depressed, schizophrenic morons. I wouldn't want to see you suffer that way. You will trap yourself in an endless loveless marriage full of misery and regret."

"Mrs. Stockton, going forward, I will consider your advice very carefully. It was very lovely to meet you. Thank you."

Then Rachel walked out the front door and sat down on a bench under the awning.

I walked outside and said, "Hello. I got the same piss-and-vinegar speech."

Joey walked in and Sue's heart was all aflutter.

"Joey, you're back, my sweet boy. Stay away from that Jezebel. She's evil, evil to the core."

Joey and I said goodbye and walked out the front door. Rachel walked with us to the car. We got in and drove to the nearest bar for a good, stiff drink.

In the first round, I ordered three shots of Whiskey. We pounded those down. Rachel spoke first, "PISS and VINEGAR, every single word. Give me another shot. I wanted to end that old bat, schizophrenia be damned."

I retorted, "Don't sugarcoat it. Give us both barrels. Believe it or not, you helped her a lot. Now, her doctors can put a face to the name. You were amazing, just what she needed. A kindhearted daughter to lean on."

"Aim at more like. She took passive aggressive to a whole new level."

"They are trying something a little different with Sue. Instead of one heavy dose of medication, she is on a very small dose of three different meds. It has gotten her this far, and we are hopeful she may be transferred to assisted living. Well, see. I guess we sufficiently survived that ordeal. Let's get some food and head for Galveston and go fishing."

Rachel barked back, "I'm all for that, hic."

We polished off a double order of wings and drove to a motel half a mile from the marina. The next morning at 7 am, we were on the water, speeding to a really hot way point. Three lines in the water and the reels started singing. Rachel was good luck; she cleaned out the reef almost singlehanded. It more than made up for Sue's deplorable behaviour. We headed back to the house with a cooler full of fish. Then spent most of the weekend eating fish and flew back to Colorado on Sunday afternoon.

Mission accomplished, Rachel met Susan, good, bad, or otherwise the deed is done. Now, all we have to do is get Sue to accept her into the family. We have time. Hopefully, the medication will help.

Joey is now enrolled in school. It's an eighteen-month program. If I'm lucky, maybe Sue will be able to attend the wedding. That would be a blessing of saintly proportion. I have been going to see Sue biweekly at the request of Dr. Demore. I settled on Tuesday and Friday. That way, I could sit in on Sue's group therapy session every Friday afternoon. The doctor was right; Sue could not stand Rachel. I could not believe some of the expletives coming out of her mouth describing Rachel. Dr.

Demore asked me to comment on Susan's monologue. I didn't know where to start.

I said to the group, "Rachel is as kind and sincere as they come. Also, she is a fully licensed and accredited Veterinarian and wants nothing more than to share the love and grace that one family can exhibit toward one another. That's all, no scheme, no plot to undermine established relationships. Rachel just wants to be Joey's companion, just like us, honey. A marriage brings loving people into the fold."

"Susan, how do you feel about that?"

"You people just don't see it, do you? She is out to get every one of us. She has had medical training. It is just a matter of time before that gold-digging skank tries to poison every one of us in our sleep. Mark my words, she will never be happy until all of us are dead and she gets all the money. She needs it to pay off all of her student loans."

"Sweetheart, I happen to know first-hand that she doesn't have any student loan debt. She received a full scholarship to Vet school. Even her car loan is paid off."

"No, it's gambling debts; she goes to Vegas all the time to renegotiate terms with her bookie. She drinks, too, a real lush. She will corrupt my beautiful little boy. Bobby, please make her go away."

"Okay, Susan, that will give us something to talk about in our one-on-one session. Who's next."

I spoke with Dr. Demore later in her office, and she said, "Getting Susan to see Rachel as no longer a threat to her is going to take time. Right now, Susan is hyper-focused that

Rachel is going to kill her. We are going to have to increase her meds again, but slowly. Approximately five to ten milligrams per week and see what happens." I told the doctor to go ahead. Then I got the hell out of there and drove straight to Galveston. I got up early the next morning and headed out on the water.

I sat down in the chair, leaned back, and said aloud, "God, what do I have to do to get Susan sane again? We have tried lowering her meds and raising her meds. She is still nuts. Nothing is working. I know that the Bible says to meet you halfway. Okay, when do I get halfway? Show me how to get halfway."

Just then, my big bait cast reel started singing. It was almost spooled out when I grabbed the rod and tried to set the hook. I pulled again, and I was able to start reeling; then, the biggest tarpon I had ever seen jumped out of the water and rolled over. Then it snapped my line. As I sat there reeling in what was left of my frayed line, I said to myself, I guess I still have some work to do before I get halfway. I stepped behind the wheel, turned the key over, the motor turned over, and I engaged the throttle. I headed back to the Marina, dropped the boat off and went into town for breakfast.

I got to the café that I frequented many times, but instead of sitting at the counter, I asked for a table on the patio, ordered a coffee with heavy cream and just sat watching the sunrise. Then I leaned back in my chair, closed my eyes and daydreamed about watching my son and Rachel holding hands, standing in front of the minister on their wedding day. Rachel looked amazing in her dress.

I have never seen a more beautiful bride. I was perched in the first row, Sue sitting next to me. Listening to the minister say the words that every bride and groom hear before they say I do. Joey, in his tuxedo, looked so dapper and handsome. I glance across the aisle and see Dean and Hallie so happy, smiling, watching their daughter on her extra special day.

"Bobby, do you want your usual eggs, bacon and pancakes?"

"What? Oh, yes, please, with butter and syrup."

"Coming right up, sweetie." I guess I dozed off there for a moment. Wow. Okay, back to the real world of how to get Sue sane again. I reached over and grabbed my coffee mug, took a sip and stared back at the morning shoreline. Sandi walked over and placed my breakfast on my table.

"Would you like a warmup on your coffee, sweetie?"

"Yes, thank you." I started in on the pancakes, not as good as Billy's, but very tasty just the same. Sandi returned and topped off my mug.

"Bobby, are you feeling okay today? You look like you just lost your best friend."

"In an introverted way, I think I did."

"I'm sorry, honey. My number is on the back of the check if you need a friend." I finished my breakfast, picked up the check and turned it over.

She wrote her number and a short note that said, "Call me if you want to talk or whatever."

I paid the check and went back to the motel. I watched a couple of reruns on TV, then I picked up the phone and called Sandi. I made a date for 3 pm. I picked her up at her apartment.

She cleaned up really nicely. Much better than the normal working kit I was used to seeing her in. We headed for the boardwalk and sat down on one of the benches. I just poured everything out. After about ten minutes, she shuffled close up to me and kissed me. I kissed her back. It was very nice. I asked her why she kissed me, and she said, "You looked like you were in desperate need of a kiss."

"I had hoped it wasn't quite that obvious. Thank you."

"You're welcome, sweetie."

"Would you like to get a bite to eat and see a movie?"

"Bobby, I would enjoy that very much."

"Okay, let's get out of here." After dinner and the movie, we ended up back at her apartment, sharing a bottle of Zinfandel. She leaned over and grabbed my shoulder, then kissed me again. Passionately and with purpose. Her soft, wet kisses pecked at my exogeny like raindrops tapping on a windowpane. I was enthralled by her spell. The next morning, she saw me taking a walk of gladness as I exited her apartment. I waited the required seventy-two hours and called Sandi. We talked for over an hour. I asked her to come and see me in Houston. She and I shared a love of country music. I invited her to accompany me to a concert on her night off. I was looking forward to seeing her again. I don't know where this relationship is going, but I know I am a very complete person when Sandi is around. My heart is very content again. She is divorced, and I am separated, but she is okay with my ordeal with Susan. She has been divorced for fourteen years and has no aspirations for a second marriage. Given the fact that Sue is not going anywhere any time soon, I can't see how spending time with Sandi could damage my quasi-sibling relationship with Sue. I don't see us ever living together again. She is still a long way from graduating to an assisted living facility. They haven't taken her off suicide watch at the facility she's currently residing in. She won't be at the wedding; Sue burnt that bridge to the ground. I still can't believe how nasty and hateful her words were, hexing unborn grandchildren. Wow. That was not a good day. I had just finished the dishes from lunch when there was a knock at the door. I opened it. To my surprise, Sandi was here already.

"Come in. How did you get here so fast?"

"I was at my girlfriend's place when you called. She lives forty-five minutes out of Houston. So, I popped over." I closed the door behind her and turned around. Sandi grabbed my ass with both hands and dug her nails into my blue jeans, and started kissing me.

Then she murmured in my ear, "You got a bed in this place?" I escorted her down the hall to the master bedroom, where she proceeded to undress me with great haste. Then she started massaging me all over. I started doing the same to her. This went on for quite a long time. We would inadvertently kiss and touch one another. We laid together endlessly, maximizing exterior body contact. It was an incredible, warm, amorous experience. I never knew how exhilarating a woman's touch could be. I assumed that she was enduring a similar experience from my touch. My climax was almost effortless. As was hers. I lay on the bed next to Sandi.

I rolled over and kissed her on those delicious lips of hers and said, "Thank you for being here right now." She kissed me back and wrapped her arms around my waist, then nodded off to sleep. I could really get used to this kind of generosity. This woman is amazing. How has she not been in a relationship with someone? I got up and went into the kitchen. Sandi gave me a bit of an appetite. I glanced over to the microwave clock, and to my surprise, we had been making love for almost three hours. No wonder I was hungry. I pulled some fresh deli slices out of the fridge and made myself a sandwich. I grabbed some chips, a pickle, and 2 bottled waters. I put everything on a bed tray and headed back to Sandi. When I walked into the room, she was lying the same way I left her. I could see her entire torso slightly turned to one side. I placed the tray on the bed beside her and gently rubbed her shoulder. She woke up, turned over and saw I made us a snack.

Then she said, "Food, oh yum. Thank you."

"How was your nap."

"Nice, thanks for making this. I'm famished. Great sex gives me an appetite."

"Me too. Sandi, I have to ask: how is it that you are not with someone? You are so kind, generous, and loving. It seems odd that you don't have a sustained love interest."

"I have a love interest, but it's not a man."

"Oh, you are-"

"Bisexual, yes."

"Wow, I didn't see that coming."

"I spent last night with my girlfriend Tina. We care for each other very much, and we have been friends with benefits for years. We are both very careful with the men we choose to date.

Tina and I have been together for over twenty years. Consider yourself fortunate, most men never get to experience what we just did. Now that you know what I am and what I am all about, do you still want to continue seeing me? I know your relationship with your wife is strained. I don't want to complicate anything for you."

"I think you are an amazing woman, and I would love to spend time with you. Is it permissible for me to meet Tina? I would love to take you both fishing in my boat."

"Typically, we don't comingle our external relationships like that. Threesomes don't seem to work out for Tina and me. She does like to fish, though. I'll ask her."

"I enjoy fishing much more if I have companions. I'm curious: how does one become bisexual?"

"Look, there's no magic lesbian fruit punch. I started off with men, but I always found myself wanting. Most men aren't willing to express femininity during sex. Tina filled that void for me. We have been together ever since. She has been with other women, but I haven't. At this point, we have no desire to be a gay marriage sideshow. Neither of us is threatened by each other's male relationships. Now you know everything. I'm glad you want to keep seeing me. The last guy I told left my apartment half-dressed and sprinted down the street. I had to laugh. You said you had a son. What's he like."

"His name is Joey; he is ex-army special forces. He got injured and received a full medical discharge. He is currently enrolled in culinary school. He lives with his fiancée's parents in Denver. I know it seems like an oxymoron, but he is really a phenomenal cook. My wife lost our first child in the third trimester. We were already having problems by then. That just complicated the situation even more. Joey's fiancée, Rachel, is amazing. She is a veterinarian in Colorado Springs. They plan to get married after he graduates. Now you know everything."

"Good, your son and his fiancée sound like really good eggs."

"Yeah, I am really proud of them."

"Bobby, do you want to accompany me back to Galveston? You can fish for a couple of days while I am at work?"

"Okay, I don't really have any concrete plans right now."

Chapter 16: Crossroads of Fate

I rented a car to drive back to Houston. The past three days with Sandi have been amazing. I am definitely smitten with that woman. I dropped off the rental and took a cab back to the house, walked in the door, hung my keys up, and hit play on the answering machine. I said to myself, I need to get a cell phone. The first four messages were duds, and number five was from a nurse in Austin.

I heard, "Mr. Stockton, your mother-in-law Tess Anders has suffered a massive stroke. Please call this number as soon as you get this message."

Jesus, I checked the date stamp. It was four days ago. I called the hospital. They told me she was listed as critical in the ICU ward. I got in the car and sped to the hospital. I got to the ICU nurses' station, and her attending nurse told me it was just a matter of time. The doctor is in with her now.

"Damn, I have been playing around in Galveston when I should have been here."

"I'm sorry, sir, we tried to get ahold of you for several days. Luckily, Ms. Anders listed you as an emergency contact."

The doctor walked out into the hall. "How is she."

"Are you Stockton?"

"Yes, how is she doing?"

"Not good; she suffered a massive stroke several days ago. Apparently, a neighbor found her lying in the front yard and called 911. I'm sorry to have to tell you, but I don't expect her to make it through the night. She is too critical to operate on or transport to a hospice facility. At this time, all we can do is make her as comfortable as possible."

The nurse poked her head out of the room and said, "Doctor, STAT."

They walked outside less than a minute later.

The doctor shook his head, "She is gone."

I walked into her room and sat beside her.

I spoke through my tears, "I'm sorry, Tess, I should have been here for you. You were there when I needed someone. Damn, I'm so sorry. I will do the best I can for Susan, you know that. I am going to miss the fried chicken you never gave me the recipe for. It's okay, I will let it go."

I grabbed a tissue from the table next to the window and blew my nose, then wiped away my tears.

"I didn't cry this much when my dad and mom died. I think I was actually closer to you than them. Remember the time the three of us went fishing on my boat? You caught that big bluefish; I thought you were going to jump in the water when I pulled it over the side, you were so excited. Then you almost cried when I told you they weren't any good to eat. That fish was over fifteen pounds. Then Sue caught a black drum that we had for dinner. Those were good times. I wish we could have had an easier time of it with Susan. It isn't fair; just when Sue is starting to show some progress, you are not here to be part of it. I am really going to miss you; I never told you that all the best qualities Susan possessed came from you so long, Tess."

I walked out of the room and stopped at the nurse's station.

"Nurse, do you know if anyone is following up with funeral arrangements?"

"No, sir."

"I will take care of it."

I left the hospital and returned home. I called the first funeral parlor I could think of, and then I called my lawyer. I will have to utilize my Power of Attorney with Susan. She is in no shape to go to the funeral, much less coordinate the arrangements. I will start making all the phone calls. Fortunately, Susan is the only heir since her brother died in Vietnam. Joey and Rachel will be attending the memorial service. There was no will. So, I decided to have Tess cremated. I guess I will end up doing the eulogy. Five days passed by very quickly. The next morning, I found myself in front of a podium giving her eulogy.

"Good afternoon, everyone, and welcome as we gather to celebrate the life of Teresa Wilhelmina Anders. As my mothers-in-law go, she will always be my favorite. Despite being my only mom-in-law, I cared very deeply for this woman. She was selfless, always looking out for me and Susan. She adored Joey and apparently taught him how to cook. He has her fried chicken recipe; good luck getting him to divulge it, though. It has paprika in it, that's all I know. Later in life, after her husband, Bill, died, our relationship matured into siblings rather than mother/son. Tess was a very perceptive woman. Bill left her very well off financially from his family's real estate holdings. Tess was extremely generous, donating a large portion of her income to mental health research. I always found Tess helpful. She was a little superstitious. I think that was from growing up in the Pennsylvania mountains. She did have some very clever sayings. I think her favorite was, 'My nose is itching; somebody is coming to see me.' Some of you have heard that one. Tess, we will miss your presence, your smile, your charisma, and your grace. So long, sis."

I left the podium and proceeded to the causeway to receive the attendees as they exited. It was a very small crowd, consisting mostly of neighbors. They all were very complimentary of her thoughtfulness through the years. One woman said that Tess, paid for a round-trip ticket to NYC so that she could see her new grandbaby for the first time.

Tess had a lot of friends; most skipped the memorial and came to the reception at her house. I never saw so much comfort food in one sitting. No fried chicken, maybe out of respect for Tess. Several people came up and asked me for her recipe. I told them I couldn't help them. I looked around the house, and I was amazed at how little furnishings and keepsakes were displayed. The guestroom had all the old photos and family heirlooms, but that was it. Tess and Susan were the last of their generations in her family. I know that Joey and Rachel are planning to live in her condo for a while. It's huge and fully furnished. They really don't need any housewares. I will take all of the family stuff back to Houston with me and list the house for sale. All the proceeds I will put in Susan's portfolio. I don't think Susan has a clue what her net worth is now. She received trust funds from her dad, which paid for her medical and then some. It's quite a big sum. I will continue the charitable donations that Tess started. She did quite well for herself. I wish we could have had more time together.

That same afternoon, I stopped by and saw Susan. She was in fairly good spirits, considering the family loss.

"Bobby, thank you for handling all the arrangements. I have become very out of touch with that sort of thing. I can barely navigate this damn cell phone they gave me. I am going to miss Mom. I can't begin to thank her for all the times she helped me deal with my demons."

"How are you doing with that?"

"I'm not on suicide watch anymore, and it has been almost two months now. I can actually leave the facility as long as I return by curfew at 7:30 pm. My life has structure again. For the first time in years, I feel good about myself. I have been involved in many of the civic activities here at the facility since I was upgraded to assisted living. This place is my home now. I am needed, and my life has a purpose again, which brings me to another point.

I feel like I am holding you back in a lot of ways, especially romantic. I assume, and you know how I like to make assumptions, that there have been other women in your life. I appreciate the fact that you have never filed for divorce. I talked to Dr. Demore, and she agreed that, given my financial solvency, it would be okay if we filed for divorce. Its time has come. I recommend we make it amicable; we are both extremely well healed. We don't need any financial hassles. I just want you to be happy. That's all I ever wanted for you. Unfortunately, my mental illness kept getting in the way. Go, let yourself be free."

"Thank you. I will try to honor you with that. We should exchange phone numbers now that we both have cell phones,

God help us. I can barely text, and email, forget it. Take care of yourself. I will be in touch."

What do I say after that, man that is a load off my soul. I called my attorney and had her file the necessary paperwork right away. Then I called Sandi.

We met at Tina's place. I was surprised that she wanted to meet there, given our last conversation, but I figured it would be nice to meet Sandi's other love interest. We sat around talking for close to an hour, ordered pizza, then watched a funny movie. I headed back to Houston around 8 pm. Tina was nice, and I could definitely see how anyone could fall for her. Tina was a day trader and a good one. That explained Sandi's money; I wondered how she could afford such a nice apartment working as a waitress part-time. I assumed that Sandi had plans to stay the night with Tina. I thanked them for the pizza and hospitality. Sandi followed me to the car, grabbed my crotch, and planted one on me.

"See you in a few days, lover." I had to jump in the car to keep Tina from seeing my erection. I never wanted a few days to go by so fast in all my life. I swear my sex life is like a roller coaster, overabundant or non-existent.

Joey is due to graduate from chef school in June, and the wedding is planned for July at a place called Clay's Ravine. It's breathtaking. There is a natural bridge, and in the afternoon, the sunbeam aligns perfectly, shining through. Quite a spectacle. I was very surprised that Susan would not be attending the ceremony. She told me after her last performance with Rachel that she thought it best to just send flowers and wish them all the love and happiness in the world.

The ceremony was exquisite. The dress was out of this world. It had a modest eight-foot train. The bridesmaids were all in a flutter as the ceremony began. The groom in his tail and the father of the bride gleaming like a shooting star, both desperately trying not to expose their anxiety toward all the pomp and curiosity that was about to unfold. Rachel, the bride bursting with emotion, was barely able to sashay down the aisle. Her thoughts wandered amidst the hope-filled fantasies of countless brides before her. She had not a clue to the bewildering question about to befall her veil.

"Rachel, will you take Joseph to be your husband until the very infinitesimal of you has expired from your physical form on this earth?"

"I do."

My buttons were bursting with joy and happiness. I think back to my wedding oh so many years ago. All brides have the same glow. It is her day, the man standing alongside, a mere caption, an accouterment accompanying her into wedded bewilderment. Post ceremony, the dress is laid in a hermetically sealed container, resting inside a restored steamer trunk beside other precious keepsakes remarking the day. Only to be opened decades later dawned by a much younger, eager, potential matriarch in celebration of her regal event.

The ceremony was over. The bride and groom had traveled hand in hand back down the velvety red carpet aisle. I gasped at a reflection that drew across me. I veered in that direction and spied in the distance Susan, standing on a mesa overlooking the ravine. The little sneak, she did attend. I said nothing of what I was now privy to. Susan wanted to attend sight unseen; I would not dare compromise her in that capacity. If I had not seen Sue staring down through binoculars, no one would have known that she was there that day, but now I know, and I am the better for it.

The honeymoon took place at Rachel's folk's place in the Idaho Rockies. I call it the Bristol compound. It is so majestic up there. I can't think of a better place to have a weeklong booty call. I returned to Houston the next morning and ended up crashing on my sofa from jet lag. I still can't get used to the altitude in Colorado. I woke up about six hours later to a firm knock on my door. I sat up and yelled, "Hang on, I'm coming." I opened the door, and Sandi was standing in the doorway with half a bushel of oysters.

She hoisted them up in the air and said, "You are not coming yet, but it's early. I'm starved. Where is the hot sauce and crackers."

"Hang on, I will get them. I have some fish dip as well. You want a beer or something stronger."

"Beer sounds great, thanks. How was the wedding?"

"Unbelievably beautiful, the venue they picked out was just breathtaking."

"I'll tell you a secret: Susan was there."

"Really?"

"Yes, she watched the whole thing perched on an elevated mesa about three hundred yards away. I didn't tell anybody. That was Rachel's day. Sue told me she felt bad about their last meeting. By the way, the divorce papers have been filed. It will be official in a month."

"That's good. I am very happy for you, or should I be sad."

"I think it's a tie. Almost three decades is a very long time. The romance has long since disappeared from our relationship, but she is still the mother of my only child. For that, I am truly grateful. She was my first real sweetheart. They say you never quite get over your first love."

"Is that true?"

"Truthfully, if someone had asked me that before we met, I would have said yes. Now, that flame is really starting to flicker."

"You are a very sweet man, you know that, right?"

"Pass me another oyster. I will get back to you on that."

"So, how is the sale of Susan's house coming along?"

"We have had a couple of offers. No signed contract yet. It shouldn't be too much longer. It's in a fantastic neighborhood. You would have liked Tess. I don't think she would have cottoned to your emancipated lifestyle, but she had a lot of charisma. Her smile could light up the room. That was something she shared with my mom."

"Okay, that was great. Do you have any idea how alley-tom cat horny I am right now?"

"No, but I am sure it will become very apparent in a matter of moments."

"You got that right, lover." Then she dragged me down the hall, pulled me down on my king-size bed, and seduced me to almost my physical limits. I swear, at one point, steam was running out of my ears. After that, my hapless naked body was sprawled over the nice cool sheets, and I fell fast asleep.

I woke up the next morning to find Sandi gone and my pain-in-the-ass cell phone ringing like crazy. I ran down the hall wearing half a pair of underwear. I found the phone, and the call ended. The caller ID indicated it was my realtor. I scrolled to the text message.

It read, "We have an offer of 20K over the asking price. Cash offer, as is, no inspection."

I replied back, "Take it; I will be down a couple of hours to sign the contract."

Cool, if this deal goes through, Susan will have her money in a couple of weeks.

Sure enough, nine days later, the deal was done. I tried to get the new owners to take the furniture as well, but they would have none of it. Well, everything in the guestroom was going with me no matter what. I did manage to get rid of some of the stuff during the estate sale. That got rid of the couches, TVs, and hardwood furniture. Nobody wanted the beds. I had to hire a junk peddler to take them away. The rest of the housewares I donated to a local charity. The place was empty and ready for the new owners. I think the best advice when selling a home is never to go back because there is no justification for interior decorating between generations. Modern furniture, aside from giving me a sore back, is often butt ugly.

Chapter 17: A Reckoning with Reality

Joey and Rachel drove down to go through the family stuff that I held onto. They paid particular interest in the bassinet. I told them it needed to be refinished, and I was planning to throw it away.

Rachel said, "No, Dad! We will have need of it in seven and a half months."

"What do you mean?"

"Yes, Pop, you are going to be a grandpa."

I went through half a box of tissues before I stopped blubbering.

"I am so happy for you guys right now. Look at me, and I'm going to get dehydrated from all this crying."

"We told her folks last week, but we wanted to wait and tell you in person."

"I should tell you guys something also. You know that Mom and I will be divorced in about a month. You don't know, but I have been seeing someone for about six months. It was just one of those things. Her name is Sandi. She lives in Galveston, where she works part-time as a waitress. Sandi is four years younger than I am. Now for the whopper. She is bisexual and splits time with her girlfriend Tina and me. I met Tina, she is very nice. I guess you can say I am in a very modern relationship. I haven't told Mom yet. I think she suspects, but she has shown no bitterness or animosity toward me. I think she would be overjoyed if you told her you were pregnant. Sue is in a very good place right now, both mentally and otherwise."

Joey retorted, "We were planning to go see her. We talked to her doctor about a week ago."

"Geese, did everybody find out before me?"

"Yes, pretty much."

"Fine. Anyway, I was starved; all that crying gave me an appetite. Let's go get some BBQ."

"Dad, you don't want to make something here."

"Oh, no, I'm not cooking for you, super sous chef. Now get in the car." The kids stayed with me for two days and headed for Austin to see Susan. I thought she was absolutely thrilled to see them and to hear the wonderful news.

I now find myself in unfamiliar territory; I am bored. I am thinking about calling Britt and asking if he needs a consultant right now. Maybe in a month or two, the fish are biting good right now. I guess I will head to Galveston in the morning since I need to restock the freezer. I am down to only a couple of pounds of fillets. Word is the reds and black drum are really doing well.

My phone is buzzing again. "Hello."

"Hi lover, what are you doing right now? Tina is having some old friends over at her place and she wanted me to invite you."

"Sounds good, what should I bring?"

"Just grab a bottle of white Zin. On your way."

"Okay, see you in an hour, babe."

Click.

I turned down the street to Tina's place, and there was a block party happening. There must have been twenty cars. Her house was standing room only, and cannabis was everywhere. Welcome to Counterculture USA. I found Sandi in the kitchen making some kind of hunch punch with half a dozen different liquors in it. I was curious to try it. She gave me her glass, and I took a sip. It was good. I made myself a glass. Then, I parked myself on the porch sofa. I didn't know how this drink was going to affect me. Sandi sat down next to me and gave me a very sweet kiss. It was probably the pineapple juice in the punch.

"How often does Tina have one of these shindigs?"

"About twice a year, she invites the entire neighborhood, so nobody complains. Everybody who is anybody is here. It usually mellows out around 2 am. You can stay the night if you want to."

"Sure, I would love to."

"You have got to meet Ray. He's a local charter fisherman."

"Hello Ray, I'm Bobby, nice to meet you. Do you run charters out of Galveston?"

"Yes, for almost ten years now. Sandi said you have a really nice skiff, and you do extremely well around here catching redfish and trout. Have you ever considered applying for a captain's license? It sounds like you would do very well."

"I never actually considered it. Would I need a bigger boat?"

"Yes, I would start with a twenty-five-footer with twin 300's."

"That would definitely be a step up for me."

"I am an engineer by trade, and I had considered taking a few consulting jobs to keep me busy. I could clear over $50,000 a year easily doing that."

"I will give you my overbookings to start. That's $25,000 a year right there. I hope that you consider my offer. Sandi thinks the world of you, doting that you are a real straight shooter. Not very many local fishermen are. Most of them can't pass the Coast Guard exam. I don't think you would have the slightest bit of trouble passing."

"No, I wouldn't have any trouble with that. I do love being out on the water almost every day. What happens when the fish aren't biting."

"I'm not saying it doesn't happen. In ten years, I have given people their money back a dozen times. Sandi says you never miss when you go out. It should be a non-issue. As long as you start out chartering for reds and trout, you will do great."

"I have to say I am growing tired of fishing alone. How are the customers?"

"Middle and upper middle class. Eighty percent of my customers are repeaters. It won't take you long to build up a nice following. One other perk is you get to choose what days you go out."

"I must say you have really given me something to think about."

"Here's my card, give me a call when you decide."

"Sandi, how do you know Ray?"

"Ray and Tina had a thing a few years ago, and he couldn't deal with the whole lifestyle thing. It was kind of sad. Ray is a very nice gentleman, like you. Are you thinking about what he said?"

"Yes, I am. I was thinking of consulting for my old firm, but it is very intriguing. You are right, I have done my homework charting these waters. I know where the fish are and when they are actively feeding. I will make some phone calls tomorrow. Babe, you may have just shown me what I have been looking for. Okay, is there any of that homemade punch left?"

"Sure, but watch it with that stuff, or you won't be any good to me later."

"Okay, honey, I will try and keep a clear head the rest of the night." Sure enough, the festivities started to dissipate shortly after midnight. Then Sandi and I went into the guest room, removed the sheets from the bed, and threw them right into the washer. Then we put a new set of sheets on the bed then proceeded to break those in good. I am starting to get those goofy feelings like I want to say the M-word to Sandi; I know what the answer is going to be. So, I may as well not dwell on it. At the end of the day, I don't really care that Tina is a big part of her life, but I wish we could be monogamous. I woke up around 8 am, and I noticed Sandi had snuck off into Tina's room. I walked into the kitchen and made breakfast for everyone. Then, I started inquiring about obtaining a commercial captain's license.

I had a fairly easy time obtaining my license, and more than a month prior to Rachel's due date, I was running charters three days a week. Ray was great; I got all the leads I could handle, and as he said, I was already getting steady repeaters. I was going to need to take about a month off after Rachel gave birth to my new grandbaby. They didn't want to know if it was a boy or a girl, so everybody had to sit on their hands until the big day. Of course, it being a first pregnancy, Mommy was a week overdue. Then, the blessed day came.

Rachel walked out of the bathroom, "Joey, my water broke. We gotta go now."

"Okay, honey, let's get you in the car."

I hopped out of bed, jumped into my clothes, and ran to the front door. Rachel walked gingerly to the car, slid in and we all rode quickly to the hospital. The maternity nurse was there to greet us at the door. Then she took Momma down the hall to the elevator. Joey gave all the insurance information to the receptionist while I parked the car. Everything went off just like we planned. I met Joey upstairs in the maternity ward.

The doctor came up to us and said, "Follow me to the locker room, and we will get you both into your scrubs."

We dawned the scrubs and hurried back to Rachel's room. Then we waited and waited. She wasn't ready to start pushing for another four hours. It was a long four hours. Then, finally, she was ready. The preliminaries were over, and it was time for the main event. The doctor took over and Rachel started to push.

The nurse cried out, "The baby is flatlining!"

The doctor yelled, "It's the cord. Get them out of here now!" She rushed Joey and me out of the room.

Chapter 18: Finding Closure

"Now, Tess, remember how I taught you. Concentrate. Let the fly touch the water first. You got it."

"Yes, Mommy, I got it. Mommy, how old were you when Grandpa Dean taught you how to flyfish."

"I was a year younger than you. I had just turned four. Grandpa got me my first fly rod and reel for my fourth birthday. I was so excited. Keep your rod tip down and work your fly. You are doing great, sweetie."

"Mommy, how old were you when you caught your first fish?

"I was a little younger than you."

"Mommy, how come Daddy doesn't flyfish with us? He goes fishing with us on the boat with Grandpa Bob."

"It's like I told you, honey, Daddy only cooks the fish up here; he doesn't catch them. The only thing he catches up here is his ear."

"Oh yeah, I forgot… FISH ON!!"

"Tess, you got this. Easy now. Keep your rod tip up high. Bow and reel. Back up. Keep reeling. Steady now, I have the net under it. You got one, honey."

"Wow, my first trout. Can I name him Wesley?"

"Why Wesley?"

"Well, there is this boy in my kindergarten class I sort of like. His name is Wesley, and he makes the best fish faces in class."

"That's funny. What kind of face are you good at making."

"I make a good puppy dog face." Tess started panting with her tongue sticking out and her hands drawn up to her shoulders. "Ok, that's pretty good. Do me a favor, put Wesley in the creel with the rest of our lunch. Let's try and catch a few more before we head back to the cabin, okay."

Dean came trotting up the trail to see how we were doing. He was very excited for Tess. Then, he started fishing about fifty yards upstream. Three casts in the water, three trout in the creel. There's nobody better than Grandpa.

The End

9 781965 560822